The Marine's New Family

Roz Dunbar

HARLEQUIN® LOVE INSPIRED®

LOVE INSPIRED BOOKS

Recycling programs
for this product may
not exist in your area.

ISBN-13: 978-0-373-87990-8

The Marine's New Family

Copyright © 2015 by Roz Dunbar

www.Harlequin.com

Printed in U.S.A.

Let all that you do be done in love.
　　　　　　　　　—*1 Corinthians* 16:14

This book is dedicated to Gram, Mom, Cheryl, Emily and Taylor with much love. The support and love I've received from all of them is incalculable. I love you all. But most especially to my beautiful mom, who encouraged me to write all of my life, and my Gram, whose old oak tree provided a cozy place to stretch out under and devour books on warm summer days.

Chapter One

Luke took the last nail out of his mouth and placed it precisely on the wooden beam. One strong whack of the hammer and the nail was halfway in the wood. Two more lighter thumps and it was all the way in. Job finished. One screened porch added to a beautiful old cottage on Bogue Sound. He felt an incredible sense of satisfaction and inner peace as he looked out at the sea from his vantage point on the roof. As if on cue, several dolphins surfaced, jumping playfully, breaking through the glassy face of the calm water.

Luke was pretty certain that there was no more beautiful place in the world than this lovely little town on the North Carolina coast. And since he'd seen a fair bit of the world in his service as a marine, that was saying something. He stood up and stretched, deeply inhaling the tangy salt air laced with the softer scent of honeysuckle. The warm summer breeze caressed his body lightly.

Thank You, Lord, for this wonderful day, he prayed silently, *and the strength to help others in need.*

"Hey, Dad, look."

Luke snapped out of his reverie when he heard the young boy's voice. Dad. He was still getting used to the title, and to the ten-year-old standing at the foot of the ladder. If only Luke had known he was a father. So much time wasted.

Coming to terms with the fact that he had a son had been difficult for him, but he suspected that Caleb was having a more difficult time. First the boy had had to deal with losing his mother to cancer. Only then, as per the conditions of her will, had Luke and Caleb learned about each other. Now Caleb was coming to terms with a new parent and a new home—a new life, all things considered, although he really never talked about the huge turns his young life had taken in the past six months.

"What is it, son?"

"It's those ladies."

"Luke! Yoo-hoo, Luke!"

Luke smiled at the term "those ladies" as he turned his eyes from the tranquil scene in front of him to the hot-pink golf cart bouncing down the dirt lane. Nimbly, he climbed down the ladder, wiping the sweat from his face with a towel he picked up off a table. Casually, he ruffled the hair on Caleb's head as he watched the vehicle approach them. The boy didn't smile, but he didn't pull away as he had a habit of doing when Luke touched him. They were still getting used to each other, and signs of physical affection from a father he had just met were new to him. Luke understood the boy's caution and felt no irritation. He knew his son would come around, with God's help. Luke prayed for it daily.

"Hello, ladies," he called. "Say hello, Caleb," he instructed the boy.

"Hi." Caleb inched closer to his father and Luke draped an arm around his thin shoulders, feeling a burst of happiness when the boy let it rest there.

"Hi there, Caleb!" Both ladies smiled broadly at the youngster.

"Oh, it looks just fantastic!" Katie Salter declared as she pulled the cart close to the brick terrace adjoining the new screened porch.

"Just perfect!" Annie Salter concurred as she sprang from the golf cart with the agility of a woman half her age, a wicker hamper in her grasp.

"What have you got there?" Luke reached a hand to help the elderly lady, but she waved it off, carrying the basket with ease to the table.

"Brought you and Caleb lunch. You both must be starved what with all of the work you've been doing for us this morning," Katie chirped as she began pulling wrapped sandwiches and containers of what appeared to be various salads from the white basket. Luke's stomach rumbled audibly at the sight. The women laughed, Annie reaching out to slap the source of the rumble lightly.

"Guess I am pretty hungry. How about you, Caleb?" Luke's face reddened slightly with embarrassment as another loud growl emanated from his midsection. This time Caleb laughed with everyone else.

In no time the sisters had the small table on the terrace set with paper plates, napkins, forks and plastic cups. Katie deftly poured frosty sweet tea into four of the cups, while her sister made short work of setting out fresh shrimp salad, coleslaw and several kinds of sandwiches. Luke got Caleb to help him pull four chairs up to the table while the women worked on the food. Honestly, he could not think of a better place for lunch or better company.

Once they were all seated Annie reached for his callused hand and the smaller, slightly wrinkled hand of her sister, while Katie reached for Caleb's. The boy hesitated before placing his smaller hand in hers, a questioning look on his freckled face. She winked at him, giving him a reassuring smile.

"Will you bless the meal, Luke?" she asked in her soft Southern drawl.

"I would be honored." He nodded. Reaching for his son's other hand, he began.

"Bless this food to our use, and us to Thy service, and make us ever mindful of the needs of others, Lord." He paused and continued with a twinkle in his eyes. "And thanks for the company of two such beautiful women and my son. I am truly blessed three times over, Lord. Amen."

The two elderly women giggled like young girls and Annie squeezed his hand in response.

"Ah, Luke Barrett, if I were twenty years younger you'd be in trouble!" Annie proclaimed, her sparkling brown eyes taking him in appreciatively.

Her sister snorted. "More like forty years younger.

And even then you'd be a…what do they call it nowadays?"

"Cougar. I'd be a cougar, which I don't mind being at all!" Annie declared with a spirited nod, almost dislodging the wide-brimmed straw hat that covered her blue-gray hair.

Luke choked on the bite of the ham-and-cheese sandwich he was eating. Katie absentmindedly began pounding on his back, her attention still focused on Annie. Caleb was following the conversation with a great deal of interest, his blue eyes moving from one adult to another as he dug into the food as though he was starving.

"Annie May Salter!"

"Oh, like you never thought of it." Annie laughed at her sister's scandalized expression.

"Well, yes, but good manners dictate that you do not voice such thoughts aloud. And there are young ears present." Katie tried to be prim, but Luke noticed she was close to laughter, as well. He also noticed she was still thumping on his back.

"I'm fine, Miss Katie," he assured her.

"Sure?" she asked kindly, giving his back a couple more wallops for good measure.

Luke nodded. "Yes, ma'am." Gently, he led the topic in another direction by asking, "When do the new tenants arrive?" Luke knew the cottage was rented out to vacationers each summer season.

Miss Katie frowned slightly, her eyes focused on a hummingbird that was flitting gracefully among the flowers of a nearby scarlet hibiscus bush. "Tenant," she corrected. "That poor girl," she added softly. "She should be here sometime today or this evening. She's driving down from Raleigh."

"She just needs a little R & R and TLC," Annie asserted firmly. "She'll be right as rain in no time. Isn't that what you marines call it, Luke? R & R?"

"Yes, ma'am, rest and relaxation," Luke confirmed as he leaned back in his chair, stretching his long legs in front of him. "Although we don't use TLC very often at all," he said with a crooked grin. He couldn't imagine telling his troops they needed tender loving care, no matter what condition they were in.

"The cottage won't be rented out for quite some time," Annie said. "Tess has been invited to use it as long as she likes. That's why we added the screened porch. Thought it would be a comfy spot to curl up and read on rainy days."

"Well, she is family, after all, and Swansboro is the perfect spot for her right now. I reckon she'll be glad to get away for a while." Katie began packing the hamper with the remains of the lunch as she spoke, then stopped when she noticed Caleb eating another sandwich.

"Extended family, but family is family," Annie amended. "Sister! Perhaps you should ask our guests if they are finished before taking their meal away from them." Annie looked pointedly at the little boy, who was wolfing down his second sandwich with a great deal of relish.

"Family?" Luke asked, wondering about this mysterious tenant. "Is it someone I know?" He wasn't related to the sisters, but they'd adopted him so thoroughly into their lives and their hearts ever since he'd moved to town that he felt like part of their family. Given his own troubled background, it was a feeling he relished.

"No, dear, you haven't met her," Katie answered. "Tess is Livie's sister-in-law."

Luke nodded in understanding. Livie was the sisters' grandniece—a sweet girl who Luke had known for the past few years, along with her husband, Adam, and her adorable twin daughters, named after the Salter sisters. "This Tess is Adam's sister?" he asked.

"That's right. We love Livie and Adam, and by extension, we love Tess. Just like we love you, Luke. And now we have Caleb to love." She flashed the boy a warm, grandmotherly smile.

Caleb stopped eating, looking at Katie curiously. "How can you love me if you don't really know me?" The question was honest and straightforward, but neither of the sisters was taken aback. Katie's answer was honest and straightforward in return.

"We chose to love you and we have plenty to go around. No sense in letting it just sit there and go to waste."

"Yep." Annie nodded. "Don't fight it, kid. Just go with the flow."

God bless both of you, Luke thought. He watched his son closely, gauging his reaction to their words. Caleb seemed to be considering what they had said, then shrugged his shoulders, accepting it without question.

"Okay. Thank you for choosing to love me." Then he went back to finishing his lunch, the conversation obviously over for him. But not for Katie, who had been watching him carefully.

"You're quite welcome. Would you like some more shrimp salad, Caleb? I don't think your daddy feeds you enough."

"No thank you, ma'am. I'm full now. And my dad feeds me good. I just get really hungry sometimes." He hesitated before adding, "Dad, can I go sit on the dock and watch the dolphins?"

"Yes, you can. Remember the rules, though. No touching the boat, got it?"

"Got it," Caleb affirmed as he grabbed the chocolate chip cookies that Annie handed him, then raced across the yard to the long weathered dock that jutted into the sound. "Thanks for lunch!" he yelled back over his shoulder.

"Ladies, that was the best lunch we've had since you made us lunch last weekend." Looking at Annie, Luke winked, and she blushed to the roots of her shiny blue-gray hair.

"I declare, Luke Barrett, you are a pure scamp!" she twittered happily.

Katie scowled at her twin sister, shaking her head as she tossed the empty paper plates into a plastic bag she had taken out of the hamper.

"Annie, you are far too old to twitter and simper," she declared. "Besides which, we have places to go, people to see and many things to accomplish in the next few hours. And what's this about the boat?" She turned her attention back to Luke.

"It appears that he and Joey Mason have been taking a boat and going over to Shackleford Island without permission. Joey's dad caught them yesterday, tying up at the dock in front of his house, and read them the riot act. Seems this wasn't the first time. Caleb and I had a long talk last night."

Or at least, they'd spent a long time in the same room with Luke doing a lot of talking. Caleb hadn't had much to say—which was par for the course. Luke just didn't know how to connect with the boy. He felt as if he was still searching for his footing when it came to being a father. Maybe because he'd never really had a father of his own. At least Caleb seemed to have bonded with Joey Mason. Caleb needed someone he could talk to— someone who could make him laugh and relax and enjoy life in North Carolina.

Luke just wished that someone could be him.

"Just being boys. Besides, Joey knows how to handle a boat. He was raised in a fishing village, for goodness' sake."

Luke knew that Annie was trying to make light of the incident, but he had been scared out of his mind when Joe had called him. Anything could happen on the water.

"I respect what you're saying, Miss Annie, but I disagree. Joey may know what he's doing, but he just isn't big enough to handle the boat by himself if something goes wrong, and Caleb doesn't know enough to be able to help. Joey isn't allowed to take the boat out without an adult, and now Caleb knows the ground rules, as well. They're only ten years old."

"He's right, sister," Katie agreed. "Now come, we need to get moving."

Not for the first time Luke marveled at the energy the sisters exuded. They were all light and motion, rarely slowing down even for an instant. Well into their seventies, they had more vim and vigor than most women thirty years younger. He blessed the day he had met them, after he had attended his first church service in town over four years ago. They had taken to him immediately and had drawn him into the fellowship of the church and the easy pace of life in the quaint fishing village that he had come to love. He felt a sense of family with them, something he had sorely missed, first in his troubled childhood, then later in his vagabond life as a marine. Something he was desperate to give to his newfound son.

Each time he had deployed, they welcomed him back with open arms and home-cooked meals. Home. Yes, Swansboro was home now, as close to home as any place he had known, and he was determined that this was where he would raise his boy. And he was more than happy to take on any little task he could to show his appreciation for his home, and the family that had all but adopted him.

"Miss Katie, do you have that list for me?" he asked as he jumped to his feet to help clear the last of the containers from the table.

Katie handed him a sheet of note paper, where she'd jotted things that they had asked him to do before the end of the day.

"Luke, if you wouldn't mind stocking the pantry we

would greatly appreciate it. I've added a small number of items you can pick up at the Piggly Wiggly. Here's the money," she said, reaching into the pocket of her flowered pedal pushers and pulling out several large bills. Luke waved the money away, shaking his head.

"I've got it," he assured her. "You and Miss Annie just take care of what you have to do. If you can think of anything else you need, just give me a call on my cell phone. Caleb and I are free for the rest of the day."

"Are you sure?" Annie squinted slightly, the sun in her eyes as she looked up at him. "Luke, you need to let us pay you for all you've done this past week, helping us get Moon Gate Cottage ready for Tess."

After picking up the wicker hamper, he walked the ladies to the cheerful golf cart and stowed the basket safely in the back. "Yes, ma'am, I'm positive, and please don't mention money again. It's my pleasure to help. We'll get the chairs and tables moved onto the screened porch and run up to the market to get provisions for your guest," he assured them. "Where are you off to next?"

"First stop is Praise Bee to pick up a gift for Tess, then off to the mayor's office to put in our two cents' worth about the Fourth of July festival." Katie neatly positioned a pair of black-and-white zebra-striped sunglasses on the bridge of her nose as she spoke, looking at Luke over the rims.

"You have a wonderful child there, Luke. I'm so glad you found each other." Annie climbed into the cart as she spoke.

Luke looked across the yard to his son, who was

lying on the dock, munching cookies and watching the dolphins, which were putting on quite a show today.

"Thank you, Miss Annie. He's a good kid. Things have been a little rocky here and there, but like a creek going downhill, we'll find our way. I just wish his mother had told me about him years ago."

"Well, you know now and that's all that counts. I'm glad that she stipulated in her will that he was to go to you if anything happened to her. And she named him Caleb Barrett, using your last name. I think in the end, she tried to do the right thing." Annie reached out and touched Luke's cheek as she spoke, her brown eyes filled with compassion for the tragic death of a young woman she had never met.

"She did. I regret not having him in my life sooner, though."

Katie shook her head. "You can't live with regrets, Luke. You take the hand God deals and make the most of it. You have him now, and what a wonderful gift your child is."

Luke nodded, a lump forming in his throat at their kind words.

"And don't forget about the breakfast after church tomorrow. You will be there, Luke? Sarah is making that delicious breakfast casserole that you so love." Katie paused, taking a breath as if considering her next words carefully. "She's been asking about you. Since Caleb has been here, she says she rarely sees you. Is there something going on there that we should know about?'

Luke was caught off guard by the question. "Not that I know of. But I appreciate your interest."

He had gone out with Sarah Fulcher a few times, long before Caleb had come on the scene, but nothing in any way that was serious. Since Jen, he had always felt that his life was too unsettled for a wife and family. That was, after all, why his wife had left him all those years ago, not even telling him that she was pregnant at the time.

After Jen's death, when Caleb came into his life, Luke's perspective had taken a radical shift. Now he actively sought stability, where there had been none before. On the surface, Sarah could provide some of that stability. She was the minister's daughter, she was well respected in town and she'd had the sort of idyllic childhood that he wanted to give his son. But there was something about Sarah that made him not want to rush into anything with her. He couldn't put his finger on it, but it was there. He enjoyed her company, but not enough for the serious relationship she was looking for. At least not right now.

Both ladies nodded as if they totally understood, taking his words at face value.

Katie pushed her sunglasses up with purpose. "Well, we're off. I honestly do not know how this village would function without us. Three thousand people and half of them don't have a clue!" Skillfully, she put the cart in Reverse as Annie blew a kiss to Luke, her eyes sparkling playfully behind her leopard-print sunglasses.

"Good thing they have us." Annie patted her sister's hand soothingly before the golf cart bounced away from Moon Gate Cottage down the shady, sandy lane.

Luke shook his head, smiling as he watched their departure. *It's a good thing we* do *have you,* he thought. Looking at the list in his hand, he called for Caleb to come with him before making his way to his truck to do the shopping.

Tess drank in the view as she crossed the bridge that led into the charming hamlet of Swansboro. Large brown pelicans flew in lazy circles near the bridge before veering off toward a sun-bleached wooden dock to her right. Several men sat on benches in front of the boats, mending nets and throwing small silver fish to the birds from buckets sitting near their feet. To her left a number of miniature lush green islands dotted the water. She turned off the air conditioner in the car and rolled down the windows, her senses delightfully assaulted by the scent of fresh salty air combined with the vibrant perfume of the white, pink and red oleander that lined the narrow street she had just turned onto.

She could easily see gentle, kind Livie growing up in this beautiful seaside town. The place was storybook perfect, and for the first time in months, Tess genuinely smiled, feeling innumerable layers of stress and pain begin to dissolve, at least a little. Her experiences overseas had wounded her in body and spirit. Both sets of injuries were slow to heal. But coming to this town to rest and recover was helping her already. It was a beginning and she would take what she could get.

Her first order of business was to get directions to the house. She had told Livie she would call the aunts when she got to Swansboro, but she wanted to do this on her own. She was glad that Livie had given her a key.

There was no need to bother anyone. Besides, there had been too much fussing over her and doing for her lately, and she wanted to establish her independence again—something she had sorely missed the past eight months.

Spying the police station on a nearby corner, she pulled into an empty parking spot and reached for the aluminum cane that had been her constant companion since she had finished rehab. With some difficulty she stood up, leaning heavily on it. Her left leg was sore and stiff from the three hour drive, but she managed to keep her balance as she made her way slowly into the building.

"Can I help you?" The bald, portly man behind the outsize oak desk seemed distracted by something on the floor as he glanced up quickly at Tess, then back to the vicinity of his feet. She couldn't see what the distraction was, but the man seemed very anxious about something down there.

"Yes, I'm looking for this address." As Tess tried to hand him the paper, the man yelped and jumped to his feet. Startled, she moved back a few steps, wobbling as she grasped the cane firmly to keep from falling.

"Are you all right?" Surprise mingled with concern in her voice.

As he moved to the center of the room, shaking his leg, Tess spied the problem. A small turtle had attached itself to the police officer's pant leg. Determination glinted in the turtle's beady black eyes as the beak-like mouth maintained its firm grip, unwilling to release its prey until it had brought him down.

"Snapping turtle," the officer puffed, continuing his awkward dance around the little room.

"Are you hurt?" For the life of her, Tess could not figure out how to help the poor man.

"No, just has the pant leg, not the skin."

"Maybe if you tried to pull it off with your hands?" she ventured, on the verge of laughter as the dance became more comical by the second. For a big man he certainly could move.

"Not a good idea. Don't want to rip the uniform."

"Of course not," Tess murmured, as she watched the duel between the man and the little snapping turtle continue.

This was just too funny and she worked hard to keep her face free of any expression other than polite concern. She had to admit she had smiled more since she had arrived in this picturesque town than she had in the past eight months combined. Maybe Livie was right.

With one more mighty shake of his leg the officer managed to dislodge the gray-green turtle, which landed with a thud next to a shiny metal bench. He immediately went over to check the reptile to make sure it was not hurt. The turtle stared at them both accusingly and snapped its powerful little jaws once more, as if to make a point.

"Aw, he's just fine. Good thing he's a baby or I'd have never gotten the little critter off me. Fierce animals."

"Is he a pet?"

"Well, now, I suppose you could say he was for about twelve hours or so. My wife found him in my son's room this morning in a box, with a whole head of lettuce sitting next to him. Boy brings home every creature he finds." The policeman shook his head, smiling broadly. "The wife threw out the lettuce, I got the turtle and the kid got another lecture on appropriate pets. It's all good. Just can't figure out how he got out of the box."

"Are you sure he didn't bite you?" Tess asked with concern. Animal bites could become easily infected.

"A small nip on the leg. No big deal."

"I can look at it if you like," she offered.

"You a doc?" He glanced at her with interest as he sat down behind the desk.

"No, physician assistant."

"Close." He seemed impressed. "Are you in town to apply for a position at the clinic? It'd be nice to finally get someone qualified in there. Real shame it's only open every other Monday."

Tess felt a brief stab of panic at the thought of working again. She was not sure she could ever go back to practicing medicine, no matter how much she loved what she did. She just didn't have the heart for it any longer. She only wanted to forget, and that was an exercise in futility when the pain in her leg and the heavier pain in her heart reminded her each day. She used to believe that God had a plan for everyone. Not anymore. God hadn't been there on that awful day, and if that was His plan, she could well do without it. She cleared the lump that had formed in her throat, before speaking.

"Sorry, but no. I do hope you find someone, though. Actually, I'm looking for directions to this address. Can you help me?" She handed the paper to the officer again.

The dull ache in her leg reminded her that she had been standing on it a little too long.

"Sure can." Taking the sheet, he glanced at it briefly. "You're almost there. Just make a right at the next block and follow the road all the way to the end. Take the dirt road to your left and you'll be there. It's right on the water." He looked at her thoughtfully. "Beautiful place, Moon Gate Cottage. You must be renting?"

"Something like that." The cottage was actually Livie and Adam's. From what her sister-in-law had told her, it was part of a cluster of cottages built by Livie's great-grandparents as rental properties in the 1930s. Apparently, everyone in the family owned one of them now, but they were frequently rented out during the summer.

The policeman probably knew Livie—and definitely knew the aunts—so if Tess was going to have peace and quiet for the next few hours, she'd likely be best served by keeping her personal business private for now. Otherwise, if what she'd heard about Annie and Katie Salter was true, they'd be rushing over to make a fuss about her arrival.

"Well, my name is Joe Mason. If you need any help just call the station." He quickly scribbled a number on the paper, slanting a quick glance at her cane.

"Tess Greenwood." Extending her hand, she thanked him. "I hope the turtle finds a good home." She couldn't hide her smile as she remembered the frantic dance the large man had done a few minutes ago.

"He will. He's going straight back to the marsh near

the river where he belongs. Just need to get him and me there all in one piece."

The officer moved to open the door for her and walked her to her car, keeping pace with her stiff movements.

"I mean it. If you need anything, please don't hesitate to call. We're a small community and we take care of each other."

The sincerity in his voice was obvious and Tess did not doubt for an instant that he meant what he said, but the offer of help grated on her nerves. Everyone wanted to help and she was grateful, yet so irritated by the offers. She was not helpless. Better not to say anything at all. Besides, all she wanted right now was to put her leg up and take a nap. Suddenly, she was very tired.

"Thanks again." She gave a small wave as she put the car in Reverse and headed in the direction of the cottage.

Less than ten minutes later Tess was sitting in her car looking at one of the most invitingly charming bungalows she had ever seen. From the blue-green patina of the aged copper roof to the pastel yellow paint that seemed to lovingly caress the outside walls, the place was enchanting. Several steps led to a wide front porch, which hosted the obligatory hanging flower baskets and rocking chairs that were so common at the homes in the village.

But this cottage went a step further. The white porch swing attached to the veranda roof was moving lazily with the gentle breeze. A colorful flag sporting a dolphin flapped gently from its perch on one of the white pillars that supported the porch. The velvety green yard was surrounded by a neat white picket fence. At the end of the driveway, directly in front of her, was a low stone wall covered in ivy and attached to the end of the house. The wall had a higher circular opening in the center that appeared to lead to a superbly tended garden.

The moon gate. Livie had told her about it. Legend had it that people who walked through a moon gate together, especially young lovers and honeymooners, were blessed with good luck. The sloping roof of the gate represented the half moon of Chinese summers, and each tile on it stood for long life, serenity and peace. But it was the view beyond the garden that caused Tess to catch her breath. Like the frame on a fine work of art, the round gate perfectly outlined the water glistening serenely a short distance away.

Entering the house, Tess drank it all in like a parched traveler at the end of a long desert crossing. *Tranquillity* was not a strong enough word to describe the place her sister-in-law had sent her to. Calm, quiet, zen, harmony and serenity were all apt descriptions. But there was something more in this special spot. *Love* immediately came to mind. It was obvious that the cottage had always been well loved. That showed everywhere she looked. The place was a peaceful oasis that was just what the doctor ordered for helping to heal a desperately hurt soul. At least Tess hoped so.

She wasn't really concerned with the physical pain she was in. The leg would heal, leaving her with perhaps a slight limp or a nagging ache on rainy days. It was her faith she was worried about. She couldn't seem to find her faith in God since that awful day. He had always been so much a part of her and now He just wasn't there. She had given each day to Him. She had always given Him credit for all that happened in her life, good and bad. Bad things happened for a reason, she knew. God had a plan, always. But it defied logic that He would abandon a group of innocent children on the day they needed Him most.

She had no doubt that He was still here, still in this world where good and bad things happened. She just could not summon the strength that would bring her back to Him. Not right now. She was too angry. Would this place help her to find her way back to spiritual peace? Time would tell.

With a grateful sigh, she sank into a large overstuffed blue-and-white-striped chair, propping her leg on the ottoman in front of it. Bringing in the luggage could wait. Exploring further could also wait. Grabbing her cell phone out of her bag, she sent a quick text to Livie, simply saying Thank you, and received an equally simple and quick We love you in return.

Closing her eyes, Tess leaned her head back against the comfy chair. No better place for a quick nap. Exhausted by the day's events and encouraged by the relief in her leg, she gently slid into sleep and began to dream.

Chapter Two

Though Tess fell asleep with a smile on her face, the smile soon faded as she was pulled back into the same horrible dream that had haunted her for months. The dream that replayed those awful events in Afghanistan.

The day had started so well. She and her team had been welcomed warmly when they'd arrived at the Afghan orphanage with their medical supplies. As a member of Hope Corps, Tess had spent the past several years of her life bringing medical relief to underprivileged countries. That day had seemed just like any other. But then it had all gone horribly wrong.

She had just finished vaccinating the four-year-old girl in front of her and was handing her a wrapped piece of candy when she felt the first explosion. Forcefully, she was sucked out of her chair as she instinctively reached for the child, gathering her close. As the air pressure equalized she fell to the floor, tucking the child beneath her in an attempt to shield her from whatever was happening around them.

*Acrid smoke began to fill the room, making it diffi-
cult to breathe. Dimly, she heard the frightened cries
of children and the urgent voices of several adults who
were making an effort to comfort them. Tess slowly
raised her head, scanning the room. It was difficult to
see through the smoke, but she could make out glass
everywhere. Glass and chaos. Both covered the room
like fine glitter. Several women dressed in loose-fitting
burkas were lying on the ground, crying and speaking
rapidly in Farsi as they began to get up from where
they had been thrown. Two of them started to gather
children and usher them out of the room as quickly as
possible. Where they were going, Tess had no idea, but
she realized it was probably not a good idea to stay
where she was. She felt a small wiggle beneath her and
heard a faint whimper. The child was struggling fee-
bly to get free. Tess looked down into wide brown eyes
filled with fear.*

*"Are you all right?" she asked the little girl in stilted
Farsi, and was reassured by the slight nod she received
in response.*

*Mentally, she went over the layout of the orphan-
age, trying desperately to remember if there was an
exit nearby. Where were her coworkers? Was anyone
hurt? If so she needed to give medical aid quickly. Her
thoughts were a jumbled mix. Taking a deep breath she
murmured a brief prayer.* Dear Lord, please help me
to think clearly.

*Immediately a sense of calm came over her as her
thoughts cleared. Pushing herself up to a sitting position, she caught the eye of one of the Afghan women,*

who rushed over to take the little girl from her. As Tess was handing the youngster over, the second explosion sounded and the world caved in on top of them. The startled look of the woman who had just taken the little girl into her arms was the last thing Tess saw before losing consciousness.

To this day, she still didn't know how long she'd spent lying there. In her dream, the transition was seamless. One moment, she was watching the world collapse around her. In the next moment, she heard a voice speaking over her head.

"She's alive." Tess heard the words before opening her eyes. *The voice was deeply male and unfamiliar.*

Who's alive? Me? Am I? I don't feel alive, *she thought fuzzily, trying to make sense of what was being said above the incessant ringing in her ears. She struggled to open her eyes without success, opting gratefully for the blessed darkness that enveloped her again. She awoke to the sound of the same warm male voice, which seemed to wrap around her like a comforting blanket.*

"Ma'am, hold on. United States Marines, and we are going to get you out of here." The rich voice rumbled close to her ear. "Morgan, get help and lift this beam off of her."

"Yes, Gunny. Baldwin, I need a hand over here."

Such a nice voice. Marines? *Tess fought again to open her eyes.* Who called the marines?

"Ma'am, hang in there. Can you open your eyes?"

Slowly, she opened them and focused on the ruggedly handsome face of the man bending over her. Feature by feature she took him in. His head was encased in a

tan-and-brown digital-patterned helmet, so she couldn't
tell the color of his hair, but his eyes were an incredible azure blue, set in sun-kissed chiseled features that
sported a day's growth of beard. There was something
in those eyes that made her feel safe, a relaxed self-
assurance that whatever was happening, he had the
situation under control.

"Ma'am," he said with a comforting smile. "I'm Gun-
nery Sergeant Luke Barrett. You're an American?"

Tess nodded, wincing with pain as she moved her
head.

"Try not to move too quickly. You have quite a bump
on your head. We'll get you help as soon as we get out
of this building. It's not safe to stay here." Looking over
his shoulder, he nodded to someone behind him before
turning back to her and saying, "Okay, put your arms
around my neck."

Her eyes never left his face as she lifted her arms
slowly. She was afraid to look around, afraid of what
she knew she'd see. It could not be good, not by any
stretch of the imagination. Part of the ceiling was gone.
The bright light was sunshine. That much she could
tell. And she was cold, very cold. The smoke was gone
and she could breathe, but each breath made her feel
as if shards of broken glass were grating against each
other inside her chest.

The marine gently lifted her out of the wreckage as
though she weighed no more than a child. She felt the
rough material of his camouflaged uniform and hard
body armor beneath her cheek as she clasped her arms
around his neck. Pain. Remarkably intense pain jabbed

*at her legs like a thousand hot needles piercing her
flesh. She stifled a groan as, with a Herculean effort,
she tightened her grip. He was her lifeline and she was
determined not to let go, even for an instant. She noted
a fleeting look of concern shadow his face as he felt
her stiffen in response to the hurt. With grim determination and quiet confidence he began to move through
the rubble of what this morning had been a building
filled with the excited shouts of children as Tess and
her coworkers arrived to set up their mobile medical
unit. It seemed like a lifetime ago.*

*Clarity washed over her with all the force of a mas-
sive tsunami. The children! The little girl she had held
close after the first explosion. Was she all right? Tess
looked back at the place she had been lying, her pain
forgotten. The child had been right in front of her, had
just left her arms. Desperately, Tess scanned what was
left of the room. It was now nothing more than a twisted
heap of concrete, glass and wooden beams. Impossible for anyone to have survived the carnage. She had
no idea how she had survived. Then she caught sight
of something that caused her heart to splinter. A small
arm poked through the wreckage, palm open, reveal-
ing a piece of brightly wrapped candy.*

*Tears began to stream down Tess's face. Shifting in
the marine's arms, she struggled to ask him to stop, to
go back, but her voice refused to obey as deep physical and emotional pain combined, causing her to slip
into unconsciousness once more.*

Usually, the dream ended there—or worse, started
over at the beginning, to play through again. But today

she heard a familiar voice say some entirely unexpected things.

"I thought I heard someone come in. Groceries are all put away and the furniture is on the porch. Why did you use the front door?"

Tess heard the marine talking again, just as she had heard him in her dreams for endless nights since he had pulled her out of the wreckage. His voice was always deep and soothing as he assured her he would make certain she was safe. She would never forget his voice. Only this time he was talking about groceries and furniture. *Well, that's a twist on the same old nightmare,* she thought in her dream state. *Why in the world is he talking about groceries? Funny.* Nuzzling her cheek against the soft fabric, she fought to catch hold of the dream to see what he was talking about, not wanting to wake till she found out.

Luke stopped short as he entered the cozy living room, his voice trailing away. He had entered the room expecting to see one of the Salter sisters, back from whatever last-minute errands they'd undertaken to prepare the cottage for their guest. The woman he found instead stopped him in his tracks. Stunned, he stood there, looking at the sleeping woman as if he had seen a ghost. She was a ghost, really. He'd never thought she would survive her wounds, she had been so critically injured when he had found her in the remains of that charred, ruined Afghan orphanage.

For a moment he thought she might be someone else, that he had been mistaken. But no, the same auburn hair glistened in the sunlight that streamed through the window near where she slept. She had the same fine porcelain skin, small straight nose and full pink lips that he remembered so clearly. Luke knew that beneath the closed lids were eyes the color of deep green jade. He had memorized her face and it had haunted him day and night. As his eyes continued to trace her features, he stopped at the small scar on her left temple. It had bled so much, but she had made it. Despite all her injuries, and the huge odds stacked against her, she had lived. *Thank You, Lord.* The prayer was silent and heartfelt.

Luke's mind tripped back to that day he had carried her out of the orphanage. It was as though it had happened yesterday.

Holding her securely in his arms, he knew that she had seen the child partially covered by the wreckage, but he had no intention of stopping or going back. It would do no good. His mission was to get her out and to safety. He could not help the dead, but he was determined to help the living. The pain on the woman's face was something Luke knew he would never forget. Senseless death was difficult enough to witness, but the senseless death of children was intolerable. Concern and empathy touched him deeply as he glanced down at the dark auburn head lying against his shoulder, but he needed to get her out of there.

Looking around, he mentally calculated the safest path out and picked his way through the debris. As he stepped across a pile of concrete rubble into the cold, bright sunlight he noticed the woman wince, and he lifted a heavily gloved hand to shield her jade-green eyes from the glare of the sun. He quickly scanned the area for medical personnel and called for a corpsman.

"Doc, we need help. This patient's bleeding pretty badly."

Luke gently lowered the woman to the hard, arid ground as the medical officer made his way over to them. He stepped back as the corpsman knelt next to the injured female and began a cursory examination, starting with the wound on her head and working his way down to her lower extremities and then back up to her skull again. Luke noticed her grimace with pain as the medic probed the gash on her temple gently, trying to stop the bleeding.

"How bad is it, Doc?" Luke knew her situation was serious, but had no idea how grave it really was.

"Honestly, Gunny, it's not good, but it's not the head wound I'm most concerned about. There may be internal injuries, and her left leg has a pretty serious break. Femur. Not pretty, and she's in a lot of pain. It's what we can't see that bothers me, though. I have no idea if she's bleeding out." He never looked up as he spoke, instead reaching into a medical kit and pulling out a bag, a battery-powered IV pump, tubing and needles.

"Can I help?" Luke lowered himself next to the corpsman, his eyes focused intently on the woman's face.

"No, but someone's going to have to carry her down this mountain to a safe zone. There is no way that a helo can land in this terrain." The corpsman had already inserted a needle into the woman's arm and attached tubing as he spoke. "Ringer's lactate with a morphine

*push," he explained to Luke as he worked next on im-
mobilizing the broken leg.*

*"I'll carry her. Just make sure she's good to go,
Doc."*

*"I'll carry her, Gunny," Corporal Baldwin offered.
Luke hadn't notice him standing there, he had been so
caught up in what the navy corpsman was doing.*

"No, Baldwin. I've got this."

*The young marine looked at him oddly for a moment
and then walked away without another word.*

*"She's ready to be moved now," the corpsman said
a minute later. "We need to get her out of here, fast."*

*Luke nodded and knelt to pick the woman up gently,
balancing the portable IV pack securely against his
chest. It wasn't going to be an easy trip down the mountain by any stretch of the imagination, and the less pain
she was in the better.*

*The journey was rough, but he never really gave that
part another thought. She would periodically open her
eyes and focus on his face. He had no idea if she could
hear him, but part of him felt that she could. So he
talked to her. He talked about anything and everything
he could think of. He told her about his life at home. He
told her about two special elderly ladies who had welcomed him into their lives and hearts, making a home
for him, the first he had had in years—maybe ever. He
told her about a village on the coast of North Carolina
where he wanted to live for the rest of his days.*

*Before he knew it they made it to flat terrain, and
up ahead he saw a CH-53E helicopter waiting. Luke
breathed deeply, knowing that they had made it and*

*that this was her ticket out of there. He just hoped she'd
pull through once they got her to proper medical facili-
ties. He met the corpsman at the door of the helo and
gently transferred her into the man's arms.*

*"Don't leave me." The hoarsely whispered plea was
heartfelt.*

*Luke had looked at the woman with surprise, his
eyes locking with hers. He hadn't thought she was capable of speaking or that she was even aware of what
was going on.*

*Smiling, he told her, "You'll be all right. You're in
the best hands possible. I'll check up on you. Promise."*

*He watched her nod slowly and close her eyes. The
corpsman saw Luke hesitate and assured him that
they had her and would take care of her. "According
to comm she's in pretty bad shape. We'll get her to
Kabul as soon as possible. They've got the best medical officers there."*

*"Can you let me know how she does?" Luke still
hesitated, not wanting to leave her for some reason.*

*"Can't say that we can or can't. They don't tell us
much because of HIPAA laws, and she's a civilian."*

*Luke nodded and backed away from the medical he-
licopter, watching it as it lifted from the landing zone
and took his charge away. And he prayed, just as he
had prayed for her every step they took together down
the mountain. He knew that God was everywhere, even
in that remote part of Afghanistan.*

Shaking his head, he came back to the present. He
had tried to find her, follow up on her, but without a
name to help him identify her, he couldn't seem to find

any information. He had run into one dead end after another and had finally given up. But he prayed for her each day. He had never stopped doing that. It was all he could do.

Yet now she was right in front of him. He felt guilty for staring. It wasn't fair somehow. She was vulnerable in sleep and he did not want to wake her. But he couldn't look away. Then his eyes caught sight of the cane next to the chair and he felt a sharp stab of compassion. The soft lavender sundress she was wearing hid any scars that might be on her legs, but he knew they were there. One thing he was sure of: if God had brought her here, He had a reason.

"Hey, Dad, I finished with the chairs. Can I go to... Hey, who's that?"

Luke put his finger to his lips, "Shhh."

"Who's she?" Caleb whispered.

"She's the new tenant we built the screened porch for," he explained simply, as he tried to usher his son out of the room.

"We don't have to whisper no more. She's awake."

"Awake?" Luke turned sharply to see that Caleb was right. The woman was sitting up and looking at them with shock.

"Who are you and what are you doing in my house?" Her tone was low and even, but she was obviously frightened and disoriented, judging by the way her small, white hands were clutching the arms of the chair.

Luke immediately tried to diffuse the situation. "I'm sorry, ma'am. We didn't know you were here yet. We brought groceries for your pantry."

"Groceries?" He watched her closely as she slowly digested what he had just said.

"Yeah, the ladies asked us to do it," Caleb tossed in helpfully.

"The ladies?" she repeated, still looking slightly disoriented.

"He means the Salter sisters, Katie and Annie."

Luke watched as recognition dawned in her green eyes, and her hands visibly relaxed their death grip on the chair.

"Oh, the aunts." She summoned a small smile as she shook her head slightly. "I'm sorry. I fell asleep."

She has a lovely smile, Luke thought inconsequentially. *She's lovely, period.* And she didn't recognize him. That much he was certain of. There was no spark of recognition in her eyes.

"My name is Luke, ma'am, and this is my son, Caleb."

"Hello, Luke and Caleb. I'm Tess. Tess Greenwood." The smile again.

"Hello, Tess. Nice to meet you. Say hello to Miss Greenwood, Caleb."

"Hello," Caleb muttered, before adding, "Can we go now, Dad? Joey is waiting for me."

"Yes, son, we're leaving now. Everything has been put away, Tess. If you need anything at all, don't hesitate to call on us. My number is on the calendar in the kitchen."

"It is?" Tess and Caleb spoke at the same time, and Luke smiled.

"It is. I do work on the cottages for the Salters from

time to time and they asked me to leave a number, just in case."

"Oh, I see. Well, thank you for the groceries. If you give me a receipt I'll reimburse you." The smile had faded and her voice had become distant. "And I'm sure I won't need anything else, but thank you."

Luke hesitated at her tone, but nodded as he ushered Caleb out of the living room to the back of the cottage. He was still trying to wrap his mind around the fact that that she was here, literally on his doorstep. He would see her and have a chance to speak with her later, he assured himself. For now, he needed to concentrate on his son.

"She must have been pretty tired. She was sleeping and it's still daytime," Caleb said as he buckled his seat belt in the truck.

"I think you're right. She must be pretty tired. So, ready to go swimming with Joey and his dad?"

"I guess so." Caleb shrugged his slender shoulders and looked out the window.

"You guess so? I thought you couldn't wait to get there."

"I can't. Let's just go, okay?"

One step forward and two steps back, Luke thought as he started the truck. It was as if the boy was afraid to let down his guard for any length of time. Luke had thought it had been a good day. Caleb had been more animated than he'd ever seen him since his son had gotten to Swansboro six months ago. Things had seemed to be changing, but now Luke couldn't be sure. He knew that Caleb missed his mother terribly, but Luke couldn't get him to talk about her. Would the boy ever feel comfortable opening up to his father? Only time would tell. But one thing was certain. Luke had never known that he had the capacity to love anyone the way he now loved his son. Not even his ex-wife.

Was that the problem? Had he not loved her enough? They'd been little more than kids, high on puppy love, when they'd gotten married. They hadn't really known yet the people they'd grow up to be—or that the years to come would pull them apart instead of binding them together. Was that why she hadn't told him he was going to be a father?

He could understand why she'd left him, and he didn't hold a grudge. She couldn't take the moves and deployments. He didn't blame her; being a military spouse was a tough job and required sacrifices that normal married couples didn't have to make. He'd wanted her to be happy, and she'd made it clear that she wouldn't find that happiness waiting at home for him month after endless month, year after year. So he'd let her go. After the divorce papers were signed, there was no further contact. It was as though their three years together had never happened.

But the proof of their marriage and their love—short-lived though it had been—was sitting in the seat right next to him. Why had she kept him from his child? Surely she had known that he would have made certain that he was in Caleb's life. Luke would have helped Jen raise their son, would have taken care of them both. He had thanked God every day for the past six months that Jen had had the foresight to write a will giving him guardianship. He couldn't imagine life without Caleb now.

But now there might be a fight ahead to keep his son with him. Jen's parents, Dave and Katherine Lockard, had made it pretty clear that they wanted custody of their grandson. They had been in Caleb's young life since he was born. Uprooting him was wrong, they claimed. No matter that he was with his biological father. They were going to petition the courts for full custody.

Luke had gone to great pains to assure both Caleb and his grandparents that they could see each other anytime they wished. He wasn't trying to keep them apart; in fact, he had taken Caleb to Tennessee for a visit last month. But there was no way he was going to hand over custody. In a world where it was prudent to pick and choose your battles wisely, Luke knew with everything in him that his son was worth fighting for. He just needed to figure out what was best for Caleb. He prayed that God would show him the way.

"Well, you've earned it, after all the hard work you've done today." He grinned at Caleb as they headed down the sandy lane. The boy kept his head averted and didn't reply. It was like climbing a mountain with no ropes. For both of them. *God, help us,* Luke prayed silently.

Chapter Three

"We are so glad you came to church with us." Annie Salter reached for Tess's hand and gave it a small squeeze.

It was early Sunday morning and Tess found herself sitting at the end of a dark, polished pew in a handsome old church. It all felt too familiar, too much like her memories of childhood, in the comfort of her local church. Back then, coming to church had filled her with joy and given her a sense that she belonged. She didn't feel that anymore.

She had not wanted to go with the aunts and had honestly tried to think of a good reason why she couldn't join them. But they had been so welcoming when they found out she had arrived yesterday, inviting her to dinner and making sure she was settled comfortably, that she could not refuse them this small thing. It had seemed so important to them. Besides, it didn't mean that she had to talk to God about anything just because she was in His house. She was just visiting with friends, she told herself and Him firmly. *Don't expect anything from me. Not until You tell me why. Give me a reason that I can accept.*

"I'm glad I came, too." She smiled at Annie. Well, it wasn't a lie, she told herself. She *was* glad she came with the sisters. She enjoyed their company.

"Oh, look, there's Luke." Katie pointed to the front of the church.

Tess followed the direction of her finger, but couldn't identify him from behind. He could have been any one of at least ten men sitting in front of them.

"He's the one sitting next to the woman with the bleached-blond hair," Annie said to Tess with an impish grin.

"Hush, sister! They might hear you." Katie adjusted the brim on her flower-laden straw hat as she spoke, but her eyes were laughing. Leaning across Annie, she whispered, "Peroxide. She definitely owes the color to a lot of peroxide. I wonder if Luke knows it's not natural," she added thoughtfully.

"Of course he does!" Annie whispered back, staunchly defending him.

"Don't be so certain. Men are rarely smart about such things, in my experience," Katie asserted roundly.

"Oh, like you have so much experience!" Annie's eyes twinkled teasingly as she spoke.

Tess couldn't hold back a loud giggle that had every head in front of them turning in their direction. Thankfully, the service had not started yet, and thinking quickly, Tess also turned around, as if looking for the source of the laugh. The sisters admirably maintained straight faces as they looked back questioningly at the people who were looking at them, until the minister cleared his throat, wished everyone a good morning and the first hymn began.

Tess listened politely as the reverend began the service, but she could not help looking for the blonde the Salter sisters had mentioned. After a quick search, her eyes lit on the back of a slender woman with beautiful silvery-blond hair caught up in an elegant French twist. But it was the man sitting next to her that drew Tess's attention. Luke.

He had very broad shoulders that exuded a subtle power, even though he was relaxing casually in the pew, his attention obviously focused on the sermon. His hair was very short and dark, showing the back of a tanned, strong neck that was set off by the collar of a white dress shirt. When she'd seen him the day before, she'd been so startled, and so shaken from her dream, that she'd managed to get only a general impression of him. She hadn't realized just how imposing he truly was. But of course, the one thing she had noticed was seated on the other side of him—a small boy with the same dark hair that the man had. Caleb.

They made a striking family, at least from behind. Tess could imagine that they were well matched in looks from the front, as well. The aunts thought so highly of him, this Luke who had surprised her in the cottage yesterday. They had told her about his help in getting the house ready for her, building the new screened porch, and buying groceries. He had certainly made her trip to the grocery store much easier. She had had to purchase just a few more things to round out the pantry offerings.

The service was not overly long and after a final hymn the sisters led Tess to a large community room that was set up with long tables and folding chairs. The delicious mixed aromas of breakfast flirted with her nose as she entered the room. Sausage, ham, bacon, eggs and casserole dishes took the place of honor on a steam table next to another table set up with all types of fruit and bread. It was a grand buffet and Tess suddenly found the appetite that had eluded her for months. Her mouth was watering as the aunts ushered her to a nearby seat, taking her cane and leaning it against the table next to her.

"We'll get you a plate, dear. You just relax. You're our guest," Annie said, before she and Katie moved over to the buffet and began loading a plate without asking her what she wanted.

"No, wait." Tess tried to stop them. She was not helpless, she wanted to say. She could get her own food. She shut her mouth when she could see that her words would only fall on empty air.

The hall was filling rapidly with a crowd of people moving toward her table. Her first instinct was to get up and leave. Then she recognized Joe Mason from the police station among them. He was smiling broadly.

"Hey, Tess. Good to see you again. This is my wife, Linda, and our son, Joey."

Linda gave her a warm smile and reached for her hand. "It's very nice to meet you, Tess. Joe says you're a physician assistant? They certainly could use some help at the clinic. Doc Anderson isn't able to handle the traffic all by himself."

"I'm not sure that I'll be here long enough to help out." Tess smiled what she hoped was an apologetic smile and shook her head. No way would she go anywhere near their clinic. She just couldn't do it. Period.

"Well, if you'd just consider it, that would be great. Folks are going to Jacksonville or Morehead City to get medical help." In a not-so-subtle movement she nudged the towheaded, freckle-faced boy forward. He looked anything but happy to be there.

I know just how you feel, kiddo, Tess thought.

"Shake hands with Miss Tess," his mother ordered. The boy quickly put his small hand in hers, then withdrew it just as fast.

"Hey, you're pretty. Mom, I have to go outside now. Mark said that Caleb found a snake by the playground last week and we have to go see if it's still there."

Linda cringed a little at the word *snake.* "I don't think so. You're going to have breakfast and then you can play while we're cleaning up, but stay away from snakes." She rolled her eyes at Tess.

This time, Tess's smile was not forced as she asked Joey, "So, between snakes and snapping turtles, which is your favorite?"

Wide brown eyes lit up as he looked at her with renewed interest. "Do you like 'em, too?"

"Well, I like snapping turtles more than snakes, but snakes have a certain charm all their own."

"Wanna help us catch some?"

Tess laughed delightedly at the eager look he gave

her. She knew she had just become an interesting adult in his small world. She loved children, loved working with them and being around them. Pediatrics was her specialty and that was what had led her to Hope Corps, and ultimately, Afghanistan.

"I'm sorry, Joey, I don't have my snake-catching clothes on right now." Tess pointed to the softly flowing yellow skirt and blouse she was wearing.

"Shame, I could use an assistant to hold the snake bag."

"No, you do not need an assistant. You are not catching any more snakes!" Linda Mason said as she hustled her young son away. "We'll talk later, Tess. It was so nice to meet you."

"See ya, Miss Tess." The boy called the words over his shoulder, protesting as his mom hurried him toward the breakfast buffet.

"Bye, Joey."

"I told you." Joe laughed as he nodded in the direction of his departing son. "Every critter he finds ends up at the house. Boy's going to either be a vet or end up wrestling alligators for a living. It's going to be a fine line between the two." Seeing the small crowd gathering around them—clearly eager to meet the new arrival—Joe began making introductions.

The next few minutes were taken up by warm welcomes from the fellowship surrounding the table. Everyone was so kind and friendly, but Tess wasn't feeling in the spirit of it. She just wanted to leave and get back to the cottage. Her heart wasn't into socializing just yet.

She hoped it didn't show on her face. Truly, she did not want to offend anyone.

As people slowly broke away from her and began moving toward the buffet tables, she noticed the aunts talking to Luke, Caleb and the woman with the lovely silver hair. After a minute all of them began to come toward her, balancing full plates in their hands. As they approached, Tess's gaze moved curiously from the woman to Luke, who was walking beside her. They really were well matched. Tall and willowy, she moved gracefully toward the table, laughing at something that Katie had said. He moved with an easy grace that belied his size. He was all muscle and confidence, and he reminded Tess of someone she had met. In fact, she was certain she had met him before, somewhere. He was not the type of man a woman forgot easily. As he drew closer, she looked into his azure eyes.

"Tess, this is Sarah Fulcher. Her father is the pastor at this church. And you've met Luke and his son, Caleb."

As Annie made the introductions, Tess smiled. "Hello. It's nice to meet you, Sarah," she said. Still that nagging feeling of familiarity about Luke tugged at her senses. It was starting to get frustrating. She really felt that she should know him, and was struggling to place him.

Tess noticed a change in his eyes when he glanced at her, but it was gone so quickly she thought she had imagined it. A slow smile slanted across his handsome face. She looked from him to Sarah. The woman was also smiling, although it did not quite reach her violet eyes. *Well, that's nice, we're all smiling,* Tess thought. *What now?*

"Hello, Tess."

Luke chose a seat next to her, and Sarah sat next to him. Katie pulled Caleb over to sit between her and Annie, after putting a plate of food in front of Tess. Tess thanked her, but she had lost the appetite that she had so recently found. The food could have been cardboard, for all she noticed it. For some reason she felt uneasy in the midst of the warmth emanating from every soul in the room. Well, almost everyone. She looked at Sarah again and saw pure dislike in the women's eyes before it was hidden behind a courteous mask. Tess shivered slightly, reaching for her cane instinctively as she glanced quickly away.

"It looks delicious," she said, giving Katie a brilliant smile she did not feel. She was conscious of Luke's strong arm where it brushed against hers as he reached for the saltshaker. *Please go away. Just go away,* she urged silently. *Everyone just go away.*

"It must be so difficult for you, being lame." Sarah looked pointedly at the cane that Tess was holding on to for dear life. "I mean, what a tragedy that you were in that awful accident." Insincerity was etched all over her lovely face. It was hard for Tess to miss it, but no one else at the table seemed to notice.

Startled, Tess looked at the woman. Did Sarah know how she had been injured? But no, she couldn't possibly. The aunts didn't even know the whole story. Before she could answer, Luke cut in.

"I'm sure that Tess doesn't want to talk about what

happened right now." He looked directly into her eyes with concern and understanding.

"Well, darlin', sometimes it's better to talk about these things." Sarah laid a possessive hand on Luke's biceps as she spoke, and looked at Tess as if to say, *Stay away. He's mine.*

She's marking her territory, Tess thought faintly. It was so obvious that Katie and Annie looked at each other with slightly raised eyebrows, but didn't say a word. *Well, lady, you don't have to worry about me. He's the last person I want to be around. I'm not in the market for a man.* For the first time in ages Tess said a silent prayer before speaking.

Please, Lord, give me strength. Let me be a peace-maker. Funny how prayers came to mind even when you didn't want them to.

"Yes, it was a pretty nasty accident, Sarah." Turning from the woman to Luke, she added, "I want to thank you for all of the help with getting the cottage ready. The aunts told me how wonderful you were. Also, I want to thank you and Caleb again for helping with the groceries."

"It was our pleasure. I was on leave last week, so it worked out well for all of us. Caleb was a really big help and worked extra hard to get everything done." Luke's voice was deep and soothing, and the grin he gave her caused her stomach to do a slow flip.

All right, so you're an attractive man, she conceded mentally. *But that does not mean that you can charm me like you've obviously charmed every other woman at this table. I am not smitten. Not by a long stretch.*

"Darlin', you did her grocery shopping? You never said. Well, isn't that just the most generous random act of kindness!" Sarah gushed as her well-manicured hand began to slowly caress the biceps under it. Luke seemed to tense and pull away from the bright pink nails, but the expression on his face remained composed and friendly.

"Well, I'm all about random acts of kindness."

He didn't miss a beat as he spoke, but Tess had noticed his slight withdrawal from Sarah's hand. Interesting dynamic for a couple.

"I mean, I expect Tess has a difficult time with even the simplest of tasks, like shopping, cleaning and taking care of herself."

"Oh, I get by just fine, Sarah. I'm taking it one day at a time, but thank you for your concern. My leg is healing nicely and soon I won't need this cane at all." She tapped the cane lightly on the tile floor for emphasis. Sarah looked less than happy with that prognosis, but wisely said nothing.

Smart move, Tess thought.

"Isn't this breakfast casserole just the most delicious you have ever tasted?" Katie looked around the table as she spoke, winking at Tess.

"Why yes, it is," she agreed, even though she had not eaten a single bite.

"Sarah made it. Luke just loves it. Seems he can never get enough of it," Annie added, giving him a meaningful look.

"Why, thank you, Miss Annie. It's my mama's recipe, but I brightened it up a bit by adding a few more herbs. Luke does love my cooking."

"I can see why," Tess murmured politely.

She did not know what was going on between the aunts, Luke and Sarah, and frankly, she did not want to know. All she wanted was to go home and sit on the veranda with a good book. The morning had gone from pleasant to awkward at warp speed.

"Luke, are you and Caleb coming by the house after breakfast? Mama and Daddy would love to spend time with you."

"I'll have to pass, Sarah. Caleb and I have plans to go fishing this afternoon. Besides, I have duty tonight and have to get to the base after that."

"Base?" Tess hadn't realized that she had spoken aloud until Luke answered.

"Yes, Camp Lejeune Marine Corps Base. It's a few miles up the road. I'm stationed there."

"Luke's a marine, and an excellent one!" Annie spoke up.

"Oh, is he?" Tess said faintly. She didn't know quite what to say as she remembered the last encounter she had had with marines. They had saved her life. Literally.

"Thank you for your service to our country," she said sincerely as she looked at him. She tried to hold on to a smile, but it was a struggle as a wave of grief seemed to wash over her. The marines had saved her...but there had been so very many beyond saving.

Looking directly into her eyes, he said with equal sincerity, "You're welcome, Tess."

Sarah's gaze narrowed slightly as she looked from Tess to Luke and back again.

"It's a shame you can't come by, Luke." She gave a

small pout. "Sure you can't make it? And where is Caleb going to be while you're working?"

"Positive. We'll stop by next Sunday. Caleb is spending the night at the Masons'. Excuse us, ladies." Luke cleared his throat as he stood up, picking up his empty plate and walking to the trash can situated near the front door. Without saying a word, the young boy followed suit, but then hesitated and turned back to the table.

"It was nice to meet you again, Miss Tess."

Tess was touched and surprised. "Thank you, Caleb. It was nice to meet you again, as well."

The youngster nodded and hurried after his father. Tess also stood, cane in her left hand and plate in her right. This was as good a time as any to make her exit, while Luke was talking to some men standing near the door. They had the same short, military haircut that he had, and she assumed they were also marines. She needed to go back to the cottage and put this odd morning behind her. She needed to think, or rather not to think. She just wanted to get away from everyone right now.

"Aunts, I think I'm going to leave now. Thanks for everything. You're both dears. Sarah, it was nice meeting you." Leaning down, she kissed Katie and Annie on their soft, wrinkled cheeks.

"So soon, dear?" Annie seemed a little disappointed.

Katie looked at Tess closely. "Yes, I think you need a bit of rest. Go home and change, put your feet up and we'll call you later to check on you."

Tess disposed of her uneaten food in the nearest trash bin and headed as quickly as her leg would allow her to

a side exit, far away from where Luke was standing. The
serenity of the cottage beckoned like the beacon of a
lighthouse in stormy weather. Once outside in the bright
warm sunshine, she took a deep breath and headed for
her car; her only thought to get away from the church.

"We need to talk." Startled, she jumped as Luke's
voice rumbled softly near her left ear.

Luke put out a hand to steady her, but she pulled
away as she turned to face him. Slowly he lowered
his hand, nodding as he acknowledged her withdrawal.
There was something wrong here, but he didn't know
what the problem was. He noted her pale face and
guarded expression.

"You scared the life out me!" She had a hand on her
chest as she looked at him accusingly.

"I'm sorry. I didn't mean to startle you. I didn't want
to say anything in front of the others. I just wanted to
tell you that I'm glad you made it, Tess."

"Excuse me? What are you talking about?" Her expression had gone from accusing to politely baffled in
the blink of an eye.

He looked at her in confusion. He could have sworn
she had recognized him earlier. Did she really not remember? His eyes moved to the faint scar on her temple before searching her eyes intently. The head wound.
Did she have amnesia? It was possible. It had been a bad
wound. And it was normal for there to be some memory
loss immediately surrounding a traumatic injury. But
there had been that connection in the fellowship hall,
that moment of what he'd thought was recognition in

her beautiful eyes. He was certain of it. So what was she playing at and why?

He took in the puzzled look on her face. She really didn't have a clue, he realized. He decided then that his best course would be not to force the issue with her. Instead, he gave her a genuine smile.

"I just wanted to say that I'm glad you're healing well."

Her faced cleared. "Thank you," she said lightly. "It really was nice meeting you and your son, and I appreciate your help with the grocery shopping. It saved me from trying to do it all myself. I'm still not good at carrying things with one hand, but I'm getting there."

"If you need help with anything at all while you're on the mend, I'm here. That includes grocery shopping."

"Random acts of kindness?" Her eyes sparkled as she laughed lightly.

Luke held the car door open for her as she slid behind the wheel.

She had a beautiful smile. It lit her face and he found himself wanting to see more of it as he watched it dance along the lines of her full pink mouth.

"I'm all about them, as you know." He spoke before thinking.

Oh, great. Luke, you're an idiot, he thought. For a man who prided himself on choosing his words carefully, he mentally kicked himself for being so thoughtless. Suddenly, he felt like a gawky sixteen-year-old. He hadn't meant to remind her of anything he had done. His words just didn't sound right. But she didn't miss a beat as she put on a pair of black sunglasses and started the car.

"I do know." She looked at him, still smiling, but he couldn't see her eyes now. He wondered what the glasses were hiding. An awkward silence stretched between them as Luke tried to think of something to say.

"Luke!" someone called across the parking lot.

He looked over his shoulder and saw Sarah making her way toward them as fast as her three-inch heels could carry her. There was something wrong. He could tell by the panicked expression on her face.

"Thanks again, Luke. You'd better get back to Sarah." Tess's voice was soft and low as she put the car in Reverse.

"No, Tess. Don't go." Sarah was out of breath as she came up to the car.

"What's wrong?" Luke kept his voice calm and even as Sarah grabbed his arm, so tightly that her fingernails dug into his skin.

"It's Joey. He's hurt. He fell out of a tree. He hit his head and is bleeding badly." Sarah shuddered as she said the words.

"Where is he?" Luke asked.

"He's behind the fellowship hall. For some reason Miss Katie asked me to get Tess if she was still here."

Luke turned to Tess, who sat frozen, not moving. Her face was ashen. What was wrong with her? And why would Katie want her to respond to an accident? The thoughts clicked through his mind in rapid succession.

"Tess?"

"I can't," she whispered, her small face anguished as she turned to look up at him.

Luke stared at her for a fraction of a second, before nodding sharply. He had no idea what was going on and honestly didn't have time to assess Tess's situation. She was clearly shaken, but she wasn't physically harmed. That meant that seeing to Joey's treatment was more important just now. Turning to Sarah, he asked, "Did anyone call 911?"

"Daddy did, but they're coming from Bear Creek, so it may take a while."

He needed to get to the hurt boy. Where was Caleb? he wondered, as he sprinted across the parking lot, leaving Tess and Sarah behind. Adrenaline had kicked in, as it always did when he was in a dangerous situation. Making his way behind the building, he spotted a group of people under an old white oak. Joey Mason was on the ground, crying loudly. That was a good sign. If he was crying he had a clear airway.

"Luke, where's Tess?" Linda Mason asked from her kneeling position on the ground next to her son. Joe was next to her, a concerned look on his wide face. The cloth Linda was holding against Joey's head was soaked with blood.

Luke's main focus was on the boy's condition, but in the back of his mind he wondered why everyone was asking for Tess. Still, that wasn't what mattered right now.

"She left." He didn't elaborate, but knelt on the ground next to Joey. "How's he doing, Mom?" He smiled reassuringly at Linda as he reached to take the blood-soaked cloth away from the child's head. "I'm combat lifesaver certified. Do you mind if I take a look?"

"I'm not sure how far he fell." Luke heard the distress in the woman's voice as he examined the bleeding wound. Joey was still crying loudly, and trying to get up, but Joe held his son's shoulder gently, refusing to allow the child to move.

"No, Joey. Stay as still as possible," Luke stated. "Can you tell me what you hurt your head on?"

"I saw it, Dad. I saw the whole thing. He hit his head on a tree branch when he slipped off of that limb right there," Caleb offered. Inching closer, he pointed out the branch, then peered down at his friend with interest and clear concern.

"Thank you, son." Luke was relieved to note that Joey hadn't been dangerously high up when he'd fallen. If he hadn't hit his head, he might have walked away from this with nothing more than bruises. "Wow, buddy, I bet it hurts like anything." Removing the cloth again, Luke noticed that the bleeding had subsided a bit.

"Am I okay, Mr. Luke?" Joey's little face was blotched with streaks of red, but the tears had all but stopped.

"I think you *are* okay. I'm pretty sure you need stitches, though, and might even have a jagged little scar to remind you of today." Luke smiled at the boy.

"Really? Wow!" Obviously, the child liked the thought of the scar, and the adults around him laughed with a mixture of relief and amusement.

"That is so cool." Caleb gave his friend a thumbs-up and grinned encouragingly.

The sound of a siren sliced through the air as the

rescue vehicle pulled into the church parking lot. Reverend Fulcher quickly directed the emergency medical personnel to Joey. Everyone backed away from the boy except Luke and the Masons as the paramedics took over. They positioned a neck brace on Joey and had him stabilized on a backboard in no time, before lifting him to take to the ambulance.

When they asked if a parent wanted to go along, Joe said he would drive and that Linda should ride with Joey. She reached over and squeezed Luke's hand before she and Joe hurried off after their son.

"Let's all say a prayer for Joey." Reverend Fulcher led the fellowship in an impromptu prayer before the people trickled back into the building, talking quietly to each other. The Salter sisters paused to speak to Luke.

"Good job, Luke!" Annie patted him on the back. "Too bad Tess had already left, though. She's a physician assistant, you know, but you did a fine job," the older woman offered kindly.

Well, that explained why the others had been asking for Tess. But what had caused her panicked reaction? "Yeah, too bad. Thank you, Miss Annie. I really didn't do much, though."

And then it dawned on him. Suddenly he understood why Tess had been at the orphanage that day in Afghanistan, and also why she couldn't go to Joey when he was hurt. The last time she'd worked in a medical capacity, it had ended in a heartbreaking disaster. After an experience like that, he was fairly certain, she must be suffering from post-traumatic stress disorder. It was written all over her face when she'd said that she couldn't help the boy. She was still recovering.

If anyone knew what she had been through it was him. He had been diagnosed with PTSD after his first combat tour. How could he have been so insensitive? Sighing heavily, he took Caleb's hand and made his way back to the fellowship hall.

Even more than before, Luke felt drawn to Tess. He wanted to check on her, make sure she was all right. But how could he tell her he knew what she was going through? He'd have to admit that he was the marine who had found her that day. And he had the feeling that was the last thing she wanted to hear.

Chapter Four

Tess nursed her mug of tea as she sat in the garden and watched as the first rays of light turned the fluffy clouds hanging over the sound a brilliant pink. Sunrises seemed especially beautiful at Moon Gate Cottage, and she was enjoying the calm quiet that this morning provided.

After the first two eventful days, the past week had been relatively peaceful. The aunts checked in on her periodically and had told her that Joey had sustained no major injuries in his fall. Her heart ached with overwhelming guilt at her inability to go to a child in need, but she had frozen at the thought of what had happened the last time she had tried to help one. She was honestly surprised she'd managed to get away from the church without succumbing to a full-blown panic attack. She shook her head as tears began to trickle slowly down her cheeks at the memory. It didn't seem she would ever get over it.

Think of something positive. Think of something good, she ordered herself sternly. *Don't dwell on the past.*

So she thought hard, but the only thing she could come up with was that her leg felt better. In fact, it had strengthened significantly during the past week, due in large part to daily swims in the warm, soothing waters of the sound. Rarely did she feel any substantial pain and the limp was fading slowly but surely. That was the physical part. That was good, right? Her physical therapist in Seattle had told her that swimming was one of the best low-impact therapies for her leg, and it seemed to be working. But then her thoughts tumbled back to the negative. The nightmares. They were not fading. Each time she closed her eyes she relived that awful day in vivid Technicolor.

And now there was last week's debacle to add to the mix. Luke. She felt horrible. What must he and Sarah be thinking of her? Not that she really cared what Sarah thought. The woman was far from nice, but still, not being able to help a child that was hurt was unconscionable. Selfishly, her only thought at the time had been to avoid intensification of the lingering pain of seeing so many children die. The incident with Joey had been a vivid reminder. Still, that was no excuse. She had never denied help to anyone in her life, until now. She was appalled at her behavior.

She felt that she owed Luke an explanation, at the very least. Problem was, she didn't want to see him again. Nothing against him in particular; she didn't want to see anyone. He seemed nice enough, but then the whole town seemed nice. And there was the fact that she couldn't shake the nagging feeling that she had met him before, somewhere. Perhaps seeing him again and trying to explain what had happened to her last Sunday would help him to understand what was going on, and help her to jog her memory.

Sighing deeply, she reached for her cell phone to call Livie. Tess really needed perspective. She hadn't found a local therapist to talk to. In all honesty, she hadn't really begun to look for one, thinking she could cope with her feelings by herself. Now she had doubts on that front, but she knew she could count on her sister-in-law to help her sort through her jumbled emotions right now. She'd sort the therapist issue out later, maybe.

Livie answered on the first ring.

"Did I wake you?"

"Not at all. I knew you'd be calling sometime soon. I just wasn't sure when and I didn't want to bother you." Livie sounded so bright and cheery for seven in the morning, but then Liv always sounded that way.

"How did you know I'd be calling?"

"Well, it has been over a week since you got there. I knew you'd call in your own time. We were giving you space to get settled."

Tess bit her lip before speaking again. "I went to church."

"Oh, Tess, I'm so glad!"

Tess felt an unexpected warmth bathe her soul at the approval in Livie's voice, but shrugged the feeling away as quickly as it came.

"Well, it just seemed to mean so much to the aunts. I went with them."

"A year ago it meant so much to you, as well." Livie pointed out practically. "And truth be told, it probably still does."

There was nothing Tess could say to that, so she redirected. "I love your town and your cottage, Livie. They're both like a place out of time and the people here are lovely."

"Changing the subject?" Livie chuckled softly before adding sincerely, "I am so glad you like it in Swansboro, Tess. That was the whole idea behind getting you to go there. I'm sure you've met a few people since you attended services. Have you met Luke Barrett?"

"I'm pretty sure I've met almost everyone in the village." Tess hesitated before adding, "How well do you know Luke, Liv?"

"Pretty well, I'd say. Your brother and I spend a good deal of time with him and his roommate, Mike Forrester, when we visit—that is, when they're there. The aunts semi-adopted both of them a few years ago when they started attending their church. Since then, they're always included in family gatherings. They deploy quite a bit and have been to Afghanistan for three or four tours. I can't remember exactly how many. Now that Luke's a single father, that might slow down quite a bit for him."

"Did his wife pass away?" Tess asked curiously.

"She did, yes, but by that time she was his ex-wife. He was married and divorced years ago. When she left him she was pregnant and never told him. He didn't have a clue until her attorney contacted him about seven months ago, to let him know that she had died. And that she'd given him custody of their son in her will. Very sad."

"Oh, no. I'm so sorry," Tess murmured softly.

Mired in her own feelings, she had forgotten that other people faced tragedy every day and dealt with it as best they could. Her heart ached for the little boy who'd lost his mother, and a father who had never known him, until now. She paused, hesitating over her next words, then threw caution to the wind figuring that there was no other way to say it except, well, to just say it.

"Livie, I did a horrible thing, and Luke knows."

There, it was out, and she felt an odd sense of relief as she watched the sun rise gently over the sound, casting sparkling tendrils of light on the water that reminded her of diamonds scattered on a blue blanket.

"I doubt that you could ever do anything horrible," Livie said gently.

"Oh, but I did. And Luke was there and now I have to explain to him. He must think that I'm an awful person."

The words came out in a rush, and once she'd started Tess couldn't stop. She told Livie everything that had happened last Sunday at church, from meeting everyone, to her feelings of just wanting to get away from all the people, to the incident with Joey and how she had been frozen with fear at the thought of medically treating a child. Livie wisely let her speak until the words trailed off, ending with how she had to tell Luke why she couldn't function that day.

"I owe him such a huge apology."

"I don't think *apology* is the right word. More like an explanation of what you have been through to cause you to act the way you did. It's understandable to those of us that know. I'm sure it was perplexing to Luke only because he has no idea."

"If that child had been hurt any worse, or had some sort of permanent damage, I would never be able to forgive myself." Tess was close to tears again at the thought.

"But he wasn't, and you need to be a little kinder to yourself. Beating yourself up does no good. You've been through enough. You've got to start healing, Tess. Enough is enough." Livie's voice was gentle but firm as she continued. "If you feel that you owe Luke an explanation of some sort, give him one. But seriously, do it and let it go."

"If I ever see him again, I will," Tess assured Livie and herself.

"Oh, you'll see him again. See that beautiful garden you're sitting in? Well, he's the one who keeps it that way. Let's see, today is Saturday. He should be there in the next hour or so."

"What?" Tess squeaked. "You're kidding."

"I suggest you get dressed, because I'm definitely not kidding." Tess heard the smile in her sister-in-law's voice.

"How did you know I was sitting outside in my nightgown?"

"I knew because that's exactly what I do when I'm at Moon Gate Cottage and the sun is just coming up. How could you not want to see that glorious light begin to peek above the water? It's a delightful place, isn't it?"

"Oh, it is," Tess breathed. "On so many levels."

"Don't worry about Luke. He has integrity, character and solid moral values. He's a rugged man, Tess, with a heart of gold. He's the kind of guy that always tries to do the right thing. I like him, a lot. So does your brother. Find the words, explain, and everything will be fine."

"Truth be told, he makes me a little nervous, and rugged is an apt description." Tess found herself gnawing on her lower lip as she thought about seeing him again.

"No need for nerves. He's a good man. And he's a marine, so he probably knows plenty of people who have struggled with PTSD. He won't judge you for it. Just go get dressed. Little Katie and Annie send hugs and kisses."

"Back to them ten times over. Love you, Liv, and thanks for everything, but mostly for being you."

"We love you, Tess. Just get to living again. We need our old Tess back. Everything else will fall into place."

Twenty minutes later, Tess was dressed and had a pitcher of tea cooling in the refrigerator. Not knowing when Luke would show up, she began doing her Saturday chores, stripping the bed and throwing the linens in the washing machine. It was such a beautiful day that she opened all the windows and let the soft ocean breeze blow through the cottage. Locating a vase on a kitchen shelf, she filled it with water, planning to go out to the garden to cut some of the gorgeous blue hydrangeas to put on the coffee table in the living room. That was when she heard the lawn mower.

Looking out of the window, she saw Luke cutting the expanse of velvet lawn closest to the water. Unbidden, a thousand butterflies landed somewhere in the region of her stomach. Well, he was here now. Gathering her courage, she watched as he pushed the mower. *Ridiculous to be so nervous*, she chided herself. The explanation was the easy part. She would hit the highlights without going into too much detail. Facing him was another matter entirely. There was something about him that caused her heart to beat just a bit faster. Shaking the thought off, she squared her shoulders as she made her way out the French doors that led to the garden. No time like the present.

Luke noticed her immediately and pushed the mower to the patio, before turning it off.

"I'm sorry, did I wake you? I wanted to get the yard done early." His rich, deep voice played along her frayed nerves like a soothing song. There was something about it, something naggingly familiar, but she dismissed the feeling and mustered a faint smile.

"Not at all. I'm an early riser. Would you like something to drink?"

Her words were polite and calm, and she was rather proud of the way they came out, considering that inside she was little more than a hot mess. Taking a deep breath, she motioned for him to sit with her at the patio table.

"Maybe later on the drink."

He settled across from her, smiling that slow, devastatingly attractive smile. Her heart dipped into her stomach, then rebounded back to her throat as she swallowed hard. He had no idea what his smile did to women, she was sure. For some reason, that made it harder for her to begin.

"Luke, I owe you an explanation. I'm so sorry for the way I acted last Sunday."

The words came out quickly, and she would have added more but he held up a hand to stop her.

"You don't owe me anything. You had your reasons. I don't question them."

"But I do. I question myself. I need to explain. I panicked and I'm not proud of it." She took a deep breath before continuing. "The last time I worked with children I was in a war zone and the building I was in got bombed. It was an orphanage, you see, and so many children died that day. I survived, but was injured..." Tess stopped, feeling hot tears prick her eyes. It still hurt so badly.

"I do understand, Tess. Really. I've been there."

Tess saw his blue eyes darken with some remembered pain, but then they were clear and smiling again in an instant. It happened so quickly she might have missed his reaction if not for her own experience to draw from. Impulsively, she reached across the table, laying her hand on his. Reflexively, his fingers curled around hers, squeezing lightly.

"You've been in Afghanistan."

Luke nodded, a serious look on his handsome face. "I have and it's not pretty. A lot of guys that I know have come out of the experience with some form of post-traumatic stress disorder. It sounds to me like that may be what you have. Any overwhelming life experience can trigger PTSD, especially if the event feels unpredictable and uncontrollable. It comes from major trauma and it sounds like you've definitely been through one. Have you been diagnosed?"

Tess nodded, hating the gentle look he gave her. She felt broken and his glance reinforced that awful feeling. Gazing beyond him to the crystal-blue water, she found thoughts of all the doctors and therapy she had been through crowding her mind.

"Look, no one can erase what happened to you, not even you," he said. "Especially not you. No matter how hard you try, it will always be there. You can and will get past it."

"I'm trying hard to just forget. Every loud noise brings back awful memories." The whispered words were so low, she barely realized that she had spoken them aloud. Again, the tears were near.

"And so you came here." His thumb lightly caressed the back of her hand as he spoke, and she doubted that he realized what he was doing. But Tess was all too aware of his touch as small tingles ran up her arm. She shivered lightly and pulled her hand away hastily on the pretext of rubbing her eyes.

"I'm having a difficult time," she admitted. "And yes, I came here to heal. My mind says there was nothing I could have done to help the children, but my heart says if only I had not gotten up, and had held that little girl under me for just a few minutes more…"

Luke leaned back in his chair, tilting his head to one side as he looked at her, weighing her words carefully before he spoke.

"I could sit here and tell you it would not have made a difference till I was blue in the face, but you wouldn't accept it. What I will say is that it's only natural to want to avoid painful memories and feelings. But if you try to numb yourself and push your memories away, the pain will only get worse. You can't escape your emotions completely."

"Oh, I'm not escaping my emotions. Believe me, they're with me every day. I'm a physician assistant, Luke. I should have been able to help somehow. I should have been able to help Joey last week. And God. How could God let it happen? Where was He?" Tess's voice was faint as she focused on a pelican flying over the water in the distance. She did not want Luke to see the tears that welled up in her eyes at the memories, but she couldn't stop the single tear that slid slowly down her cheek.

"Aw, Tess, God *was* there. He puts you where you were meant to be, whether you wanted to be there or not. There was a reason you were there on that day." His words were low and laced with empathy as he got up from his seat and came around the table, kneeling in front of her before drawing her into the comfort of his strong arms. "Go ahead and cry for them. Cry for you, as well, because you lost a part of you that day, too."

Tess had no idea where all the tears came from, but she sobbed like a baby as she rested her face against the soft polo shirt. She cried for the children. She cried for the adults who had lost their lives and she cried for the young woman she had been and the innocence she had lost that day. She had always believed that people were innately good, but had learned a harsh truth that had turned her safe world upside down.

Now, for the first time, she had found someone who understood what she was feeling, and it was the most cathartic experience she had ever had in her life. For the first time since she had recovered physically, she felt free to truly let her emotional pain spill to the surface.

Slowly, the tears subsided and she became intensely aware of his solid arms around her in that safe, soothing embrace. And the tearstained mess she had made on the front of his shirt. What must he be thinking? Slowly she lifted her head, her eyes locking with his azure-blue ones. Neither spoke for a minute, until Tess took a breath.

"Thank you," she whispered softly, giving a little hiccup that caused him to smile.

Luke was the first to pull away, leaning back on his heels as he studied her teary face.

"Feel better?" He rose to his feet as he spoke, not waiting for an answer. Tess watched him walk through the French doors into the kitchen, coming back a moment later with a clean damp washcloth and a handful of tissues.

"I've made a mess of your shirt," she sniffed as she reached for them.

"My shirt is fine. Are you?"

Tess nodded as she blew her nose. "Aside from feeling like a perfect idiot, I'm surprisingly good. You were right that it helped to let it all out."

"You're not an idiot. Healing has to start somewhere. I think that this might be the first time you've cried."

"In front of anyone. How did you know?" Tess couldn't keep the surprise from her voice.

Luke turned and walked to the edge of the terrace, looking at the clear blue water before turning back to her.

"I told you, I've been where you are. I don't just sympathize with you, I literally feel your anguish."

Again, Tess caught the fleeting look of pain in his eyes and thought he might say something about it. Instead he held out a strong hand and said, "Come on."

Without thinking, she placed her palm in his and asked, "Where?"

"The Lord has seen fit to give us a beautiful day today. We're going to a street fair to celebrate."

Tess stiffened instinctively and jerked her hand away from his. "No."

"No?" Luke's first reaction was to reach for her hand again. She made a feeble attempt to free it, but he refused to let go.

"I just don't want to be in the middle of a large group of people right now." Her voice was low and he had to bend his head to hear her words.

Luke watched her pale cheeks flood with color as her eyes slid downward to focus on her small white hand clasped lightly in his larger one. Again he felt her give a small tug to get free, and he tightened his grasp slightly before shrugging and letting go. If she wanted to put some distance between them, he'd let her. She probably felt that she needed to regroup after putting her emotions on display—something he could tell she wasn't used to doing.

Moments ago, he had come close to telling her that

he had been there with her in Afghanistan, but now he was glad he'd held back. She was overwhelmed enough already. She wasn't prepared to hear about his role in that day just yet. One step at a time.

"Maybe getting away from here is what you need right now. Have you been out since church last week?" He tried hard to gauge her mood. Staying hidden away in the cottage could not be helping her emotionally. Too much time to think back, reflect and get mired in survivor's guilt.

"No, but I really don't see that it's been a bad thing to be alone for a week." This time when she spoke she looked him directly in the eyes. But she might as well have looked away. Her emotional shields were back up, and he could no longer see her thoughts or feelings reflected in her eyes. "And why are you pushing? I really do have a lot to get done today."

"I'm sure you do. And I have to finish the yard, then shower and change before I can go. You'd have plenty of time to get those things done while I finish my chores."

"Where's Caleb?" she asked. Luke knew she was trying to change the subject, and he let her. He reckoned it had been a pretty rough day for her so far and it was time to let it go. "Couldn't he help you with the yard work?"

"He usually does, but I gave him a free pass today. He's with Joey Mason at the street fair. They're helping Joe man the dunking booth."

"I bet they're having a great time!" Tess gave him a genuine smile that lit up her face and made him catch his breath. She really was beautiful, and the smile only added to her looks. He shook his head a little as if to clear it, hoping she didn't catch the expression on his face or the movement.

"I know they are, and driving Joe crazy while they're at it," Luke said wryly, trying to sound casual.

That smile had really caught him off guard and made his heart skip a beat. Where had that come from? he wondered.

Well, what did you expect? he chided himself. *You appreciate beautiful women as much as the next red-blooded male... Except your heart usually doesn't skip a beat when one smiles at you.*

The last thing he needed in his life right now was to be attracted to a woman. He had enough on his plate making a stable home for himself and Caleb. His son took priority over everything else in his life, and that was how it should be.

"Somehow, I think that Joe might be driving *them* crazy." Tess had stood up as she spoke, moving toward the house. "I'll be right back."

She returned a few minutes later with a tall glass of iced tea and set it on the table in front of him. "For later, in case you get thirsty," she offered with a tentative smile.

"Thanks for the tea and the smile. You have a lovely smile, Tess," he said gruffly.

He felt a little awkward saying that, but then checked himself. Everyone deserved a compliment now and then, and besides, it was the truth. He noticed her pale cheeks flood with color as he picked up the tea and took a long drink. He was a battle-hardened United States

Marine. Compliments weren't his style at all, but here he was dishing them out. Go figure.

"Sure you won't come to the festival?" he asked once more.

"Thank you for the invitation, but no, Luke. I'm content here." Her chin lifted a little and her face took on a defiant look.

"No worries, then. This town has a festival every few weeks, it seems. There will be another time. They really are a lot of fun."

"Why do you all have so many festivals?" Tess asked curiously.

"I'm not sure, but I have a theory. I believe that we like to show off the village, as well as spend time with each other."

"The town is lovely and so are the people that I've met so far." Tess nodded as if it all made sense.

"It is and we are. Well, back to work for me." He walked to the lawn mower as he spoke, flashing her what he hoped was an easy smile, while inside he felt more than a little disappointed. He could not make her do what she did not want to do.

"If you change your mind, my cell phone number is—"

"On the calendar in the kitchen," she finished. He noted the serious look on her face.

"I can take my number off the calendar if you want," he offered.

"Oh, no. No. It's not that." She seemed to be searching for the right words as he waited patiently. "I... Thank you for listening to me and letting me cry."

Again, empathy and compassion tugged at his heart. She really was in pain.

"No problem. I hope it helped."

She nodded and he took that gesture as his cue to get back to work. There was really nothing left to say.

"Good." He started the mower and walked away without another word.

Chapter Five

"Can't say as I blame her for not wanting to come." Katie kept a sharp eye on the people milling around the church booth as she spoke to Luke. "She's only been here a week. There will be plenty of time for her to get out and about after a little downtime. Excuse me for a minute." Katie moved quickly to the front of the booth, where Annie was taking care of several customers. "Sister, all of the strawberry preserves are two-fifty, not one seventy-five."

"None of them are marked," Annie pointed out as she took the money from the young woman standing at the front of the line. "I'll be sure to overcharge next time."

There was a hint of exasperation in Annie's voice as she watched Katie roll her eyes before turning back to a laughing Luke. How he loved these ladies.

Looking around the street with interest, he mentally counted some thirty brightly painted booths selling everything from artwork like pottery, jewelry, paintings, carvings and stained glass, to many varieties of food, to hand-painted T-shirts. There were games and play areas for children, including a bouncy house that seemed to be a huge hit. Adding to the ambience, a local band in the large white pavilion in the town square was playing an eclectic mix of beach music and top forty hits. The mouthwatering scent of a homegrown favorite, shrimp burgers, mingled with the sweet fragrance of funnel cakes, wafting in the gentle coastal breeze. Judging by the people who were milling everywhere, this year's event was shaping up to be an unqualified success. All of Main Street had been closed for the occasion, which lasted well into the evening each year on the second Saturday in June. The event, dubbed Arts by the Sea, drew tourists from all over the Crystal Coast, as well as military families from nearby Camp Lejeune and people from as far away as Raleigh.

Luke was still trying to come up with a way to get Tess there. It would do her a world of good, and in all honesty, he really wanted to spend more time with her. She had rarely left his thoughts over the past week, and not just because he wanted to help her heal her bruised spirit. He truly wanted to get to know her better, to see how she had gotten on while she was recovering. That she had actually survived had renewed his faith in God, and he hated to think the experience had damaged her beliefs. He hoped he could help her with that.

Wanting to spend time with Tess surprised him on many levels. After his unstable childhood, he'd latched on to Jen hard and fast, rushing into a marriage neither one of them had really been ready for. Once it had fallen apart, he'd reached the conclusion that that brand of happily-ever-after just wasn't meant for him. It wouldn't be fair of him to ask any other woman to take on his chaotic lifestyle. While he had dated some in the years since then, he had always made it a point to not become too attached to any woman. He had kept Sarah at arm's length as much as possible, although he knew she was pushing hard to take the friendship further. A romantic relationship with her just wasn't what he was looking for.

Especially now that he had Caleb. Luke was determined to give his son the love that he himself had never had as a child. And that meant making him a priority the way Luke had never been for either of his parents. It also meant building a real home for Caleb—one where he would always feel safe and valued. At least Luke could be sure he'd picked the right town for that home. This appealing community and the warm, generous townsfolk already meant so much to him. He knew without a doubt that he wanted this to be his permanent home when he left the Corps—a time that seemed to be drawing nearer.

He could feel his life changing in both subtle and major ways lately, leaving him feeling a bit unsure of himself. For a man with a strong sense of direction and solid convictions, it was a bit unnerving.

Shaking his head, he moved the thoughts to the back of his mind. He just wanted to enjoy the day, preferably with Caleb. Tess joining them would be an added bonus.

"Luke? Did you hear anything I just said to you?" Katie was watching him closely, a puzzled expression on her face.

Luke started at the sound of his name. "Yes? Miss Katie, did you say something?"

"I did, but you obviously did not hear it."

"Don't badger him, sister." Annie smiled sympathetically at Luke as he looked bemusedly from one to the other.

He gave the women a gentle smile as he apologized. "I zoned for a minute. I'm so sorry. Forgive me?"

"Zoned?" Katie arched a quizzical brow at the word. "And of course I forgive you. I could never be angry with you."

"Went somewhere else in his mind," Annie threw in by way of explanation. "You know, sister, daydreaming."

"How in the world do you know all these things?"

"I make it a point to keep up on the current slang."

"Of course you do. Why did I even ask?" Katie flashed her a sharp look before turning back to Luke.

"Good gracious, Luke, you *were* a million miles away. I asked if you had hired a nanny for Caleb yet."

"No. Nothing so far. Caleb and I have been interviewing all week. Seems that the ones I like Caleb doesn't and vice versa."

"Cutting it close, aren't you?" Annie's soft brown eyes were filled with concern.

"Yeah, we are. Linda can keep him for maybe another week, but after that she starts her new job and Joey will go to his grandmother during the day." Luke was concerned, as well. He was worried that without good care for Caleb, his chances of retaining custody of his son in a court battle would drop dismally. Tired, he rubbed the back of his neck.

"Surely Cora wouldn't mind taking on Caleb," Katie tossed out as she walked over to help two customers interested in the jams and jellies that lined one of the shelves. "Don't go anywhere," she ordered Luke. "I have an idea."

"I'm glad someone does," he muttered as he watched her helping the young couple. Annie reached over and rubbed his arm comfortingly.

"It will all work out, Luke. Why can't Cora take Caleb?"

"She cares for three of her other grandchildren, Miss Annie. I can't drop Caleb on her, as well, and I won't even ask. That would give her five kids all under the age of eleven."

Annie nodded thoughtfully. "Have you heard from the grandparents?"

"No, not me, but Caleb called them last night to wish his grandfather happy birthday. Just glad I checked the calendar after dinner and saw it."

"You're a good father, Luke. Those grandparents will see it for themselves sooner or later. Put it in God's hands." Annie squeezed his arm comfortingly.

Luke patted her hand in acknowledgment. "I am trying, Miss Annie. I have an appointment with my commanding officer on Monday. I need to get to base legal and talk to someone." Luke's heart wrenched at the thought that Caleb might not be with him in another six months.

"It's just not right. A boy needs to be with his daddy."

Annie turned to look at her sister, who had just come back to join them. "Don't you agree, sister?"

"I won't say whether I agree to something until I know what I am agreeing to." Katie's questioning eyes focused first on Annie and then on Luke.

"That a boy needs to be with his father, of course. Weren't you paying attention?"

"Sister, I wasn't here, remember?"

"Oh, right."

Luke laughed in spite of himself. Maybe Annie was right and things would work out. He needed to put it in God's hands, as she had suggested. But not having control didn't sit well with him. He knew that he had to do everything he could and God would guide him. He firmly believed in the power of prayer.

"Of course Caleb needs to be with his daddy, and I suspect that his daddy needs to be with him just as much," Katie confirmed. "So here's my idea on child care for Caleb. Ask Tess."

Stunned silence greeted her words. And then Annie clapped her hands together and a huge smile lit her face. "Scathingly brilliant, sister! Kills two birds with one stone."

"Whoa." Luke was shaking his head empathetically. "I can't ask her."

"Well, why in the world not? You need help and she's available. I don't see the problem," Katie said firmly. Luke knew from experience that he could not and should not argue with her. But he couldn't stop himself from trying.

"She has enough on her plate right now. Caring for

a little boy is the last thing she needs. Besides which, I'm fairly positive she wouldn't want to."

"Oh, piddle. She needs to get invested in something other than herself. She needs to have a reason to move beyond what happened. I know you don't know what she's dealing with now, Luke, but trust me when I say that her caring for Caleb is the perfect solution. For both of you."

"I know a little of what she went through."

Luke felt a twinge of guilt. He couldn't tell anyone, not even the sisters, that he'd been with her the day she got wounded in Afghanistan. Eventually they would know, but not until after he'd discussed it with Tess. He sincerely hoped that one day they would be able to talk about it without the overwhelming pain she felt.

"How do you know?" Annie looked slightly puzzled as she asked the question.

"She told me some of it this morning." He shrugged his shoulders, feeling a little uncomfortable. Well, it wasn't a lie. She *had* told him, but he was beginning to feel that by not telling Tess that he had been there, he was lying by omission.

"Oh, well, then. You understand where we're going with this." Annie's face cleared and she smiled brightly.

"I understand, but I don't think it's a good idea to ask her."

Katie held up a hand, her face thoughtful as she looked hard at Luke. "She told you? She hasn't even told us about what happened. Livie told us. What prompted Tess to talk about it? Don't get me wrong, it's good that she did. Livie says she never talks about it."

What to say and not have it be a lie? *Lord, give me the right words,* he prayed silently.

"It just came up in conversation this morning, and it wasn't a great deal of information."

There. That should satisfy them, he thought as he flashed them a loving smile. He didn't quite get the response he thought he would, from Miss Katie at any rate. Both sisters returned the smile, but Katie's was lukewarm and laced with suspicion, although she didn't push the subject. Instead she said, "Well, think about it, then. You might want to broach the subject subtly when you go to pick her up."

"Pick her up?"

"Yes. Tess is coming to help man the booth."

He was caught off guard by this bit of news. "She is? Why didn't she say something to me this morning?"

"Because this morning she didn't know she was helping us," Annie said, as though it all made perfect sense. "I just called her and with a bit of gentle persuasion convinced her that we could not do without her."

"Well, you did seem to think it was best for her to get out, and we're not going to let her sit in that cottage, as lovely as it is, and vegetate," Katie pointed out, as she and Annie exchanged knowing looks.

"Yes, it is, but you can't force her. I mean, when I invited her to come here with me, I wanted her to enjoy the day, not spend her time working, or even worse, resenting that she was forced to go out at all."

Luke didn't know quite what to say and none of it was coming out the way he meant it to. "No offense, ladies," he added.

"None taken, dear boy." Annie assured him, patting his arm.

"Really, do you honestly think we would chain her to this booth when there is a whole, glorious festival full of life going on around us?" Katie arched a slim eyebrow at him as she adjusted her straw hat. "We have a ton of help here today, everyone taking turns. We don't *need* her, we *want* her here. We just chose the method necessary to get her here."

"And when she arrives, we'll just tell her that other help has come and to carpe diem!" Annie winked at Luke before moving over to a customer looking at the mouthwatering baked goods the church was selling in addition to the homemade jams and jellies.

"So we need you to go pick her up. Make sure she has plenty of sunscreen and that she slathers it liberally on all exposed skin! Oh, and tell her to bring the straw hat we gave her. She has such beautiful, porcelain skin, don't you think? Of course you do." Katie answered her own question as she gave him an assessing look.

"I… Does she know I'm her ride?" It was all he could think of to say.

"I just sold all of Linda Mason's apple scones in one fell swoop!" Annie beamed as she made her way back to them.

"I hope you charged appropriately, sister. I declare, between you and Sarah, you're giving the product away!"

"Oh, shush. Sarah only gave Joey, Caleb and Kevin some cupcakes. We have plenty."

"Humph. Plenty that we're meant to *sell*. Might as

well put a sign up that says Free Treats. The whole idea is to make money for the clinic. Please try to remember that, Annie."

Her sister just smiled placidly as Katie heaved a defeated sigh and shook her head before turning back to Luke.

"Does it make a difference whether it's you or one of us coming for her?"

"It might," Luke admitted quietly.

"Oh, pish posh! Take the golf cart and go get her. It will take too long to get your truck from the parking area. She's a good soul, Luke, and so are you. You both need a little fun in your young lives, with everything you're both going through right now." Katie's voice brooked no argument, so Luke deftly changed the subject.

"Speaking of Sarah, I thought she would be here."

"She was earlier, but then Ben Carter stopped by. I expect that they are having a wonderful time right about now soaking up some sun and fun." Katie smiled brightly. "She should be back soon if you want to see her."

"No, I'm fine. I'll see her later and say hello. You two wouldn't by any chance be matchmaking for Sarah, would you? I smell subterfuge afoot."

"And I smell shrimp burgers. I'm starved," Annie chirped. "Now shoo! We have work to do. The clinic needs cash. Stat!"

"Stat?" Katie asked, as she and Annie moved toward more festival goers who had stopped by the booth.

"Yes. It means right away. It's a medical term. I heard the actors use it on reruns of *ER*."

Luke laughed out loud as he listened to the sisters' banter. The sun, for some reason, was suddenly shining much brighter than it had been just a minute ago.

He made it to the cottage in less than fifteen minutes. No mean feat, considering he was driving a golf cart on back streets in order to avoid routes closed off to vehicle traffic for the fair.

Pulling into the driveway at the Moon Gate Cottage, he jumped out of the cart, stopping short as he caught his breath sharply. Tess was sitting on the terrace intently reading a book, seeming oblivious to anything going on around her. From his vantage point she was framed by the soft lavender and blush-colored climbing roses on the trellis she was sitting under. She looked beautiful, he thought. She reminded him of a Renoir painting he had seen at the Musée d'Orsay when he had visited Paris a few years ago. It was of an exquisite woman surrounded by flowers, reading a book. He felt an odd twinge somewhere in the region of his gut, but quickly dismissed it.

Get a grip, he ordered himself, before clearing his throat and walking through the gate.

Tess looked up at the sound of approaching footsteps and smiled dreamily when she saw him, still lost in the pages of the romance novel she had been reading. Luke could certainly be a hero in any romance, she thought. He fit the cliché hero image. Tall, strong and ruggedly handsome.

Whoa, girl! Where had that come from? Shaking her head slightly, she erased the smile and replaced it with a polite and guarded look. She had to be wary of starting to like him a little too much. She could not afford that. Ever.

Ever? Well, ever was a long time, she amended mentally. *Just not now.* She knew she had far too much emotional baggage to get involved with anyone right now, let alone a marine who seemed determined to act as her therapist.

No, that wasn't fair. By all accounts, Luke was just being Luke. It was just so maddening that he had so many attributes that she liked and admired. Would it kill him to pick up a few bad habits, and make this all easier on her?

"Hello, Luke." She put the book aside and picked up her cane as he walked toward her. "Looks like I'm going to the festival, after all," she said as she stood up.

"So it would appear." He sent her a lazy smile as he reached for her bag, which was lying on the table.

"No, I've got it." She went for it at the same time and their hands touched. She snatched hers away as if the contact had burned her, giving up the bag to his large, capable hands. She looked up at him briefly and noticed his smile fade for a moment, but then return just as quickly.

"I'm parked in front. Hope you don't mind, but Miss Katie had me take the golf cart. It's faster, with my truck parked where it is."

Tess was intensely aware of his hand on her elbow as he guided her through the moon gate. It was the first time she had walked through it since she had arrived. Remembering the legend about couples that walked through the gate together, she felt herself blush a little as she felt Luke's eyes on her.

"You know the folklore surrounding the moon gate, I see."

"Um, yes, I know the story." She tried to pick up her pace as she spoke, but to no avail. He had stopped directly under the gate and stretched a hand out to touch it.

"What are you doing?" She was curious in spite of herself, her embarrassment fading as she watched him close his eyes for a minute, then open them, giving her a smile.

"Saying a prayer, of course." He spoke as if she should have known; as if it made all the sense in the world.

"Oh, I see. I don't seem to recall Livie telling me that part of the lore."

"I can see she missed the best part. The prayer is the catalyst for all the good things to come. When a couple prays as they pass through the gate, they are absolutely guaranteed everlasting happiness and good fortune throughout their marriage."

Tess felt her jaw drop as she stared at him. A thousand butterflies landed in the pit of her stomach in response to his explanation. He couldn't be serious. Could he? Couple? Marriage? Seriously, she needed to set him straight on a few things, the first being the couple part.

"Luke, I don't know what you—"

He put his hand gently under her elbow again and steered her in the direction of the vibrantly colored golf cart.

"Relax, Tess. I didn't mean that we were a couple.

Far from it. Just saying a little prayer. It had nothing to do with you."

Well, that puts you in your place, Tess, she thought as she reached into her bag and pulled out a pair of black sunglasses, plopping them on a little forcefully without looking at him.

"I knew that," she replied for good measure.

"No, you didn't, but that's okay." He spoke matter-of-factly, with no hint of irritation or one-upmanship on his handsome face.

Take it at face value, Tess. He really is a nice guy, she told herself. *Don't read into things.*

She tried to relax back against the seat as the cart bounced down the sandy, tree-lined lane, but she couldn't manage to feel quite at ease with this man who had seen her at her worst. This morning she had been an emotional ruin, and Luke had been so strong and certain of what he had said to her that he had eased her pain considerably. But despite his comforting words earlier, she couldn't help but feel silly for breaking down like that in front of him. And then she had misread his comments under the moon gate, to top off the bad impression she was making on the man. She felt like a fool. What he was thinking of her, she hadn't a clue, but it couldn't be that she was a stable human being, not by a long shot. She wished he hadn't been the one to come pick her up.

On the other hand, part of her was glad that the aunts had called to ask for her help, forcing her to leave the cottage. She was coming to realize that being alone was not a good place anymore. In fact, it was becoming more difficult to tolerate. But she was finding it hard to take the first steps to letting go. If only the nightmares would go away. If only she could reconcile herself to God's will on that day. She had never been the type of person to live with regrets about anything, until this past year.

Don't overanalyze the situation, she told herself sternly. *Just enjoy the fine day. Let yourself be happy today, Tess, please,* she begged herself.

Chapter Six

"**D**id you slather?" Luke tossed the question at her casually as he negotiated the narrow, paved streets.

"Excuse me?"

"I was instructed to make sure that you slathered yourself with sunblock." He grinned as he glanced over at her.

"Oh! The aunts?" Tess laughed at the terminology.

Slather was a good word for how she had applied the lotion. A sunburn was the last thing she wanted or needed. She was wearing a sleeveless, crisp white cotton blouse and black cotton capris, with strappy white sandals. She loved the sun, but always had to protect her fair skin from its harsh rays during the summer months. One painful burn as a teen had indelibly impressed the need to protect herself forever after.

"Yep. Miss Katie was very concerned about your skin."

"How kind of her to even think about it! Yes, I am duly slathered and have more lotion in my bag."

"Good. I almost forgot to mention it. So we have lotion."

"Check," Tess affirmed.

"Hat."

"Check."

"Money for incidentals?"

"Oops, no. We need to go back." Tess had totally forgotten to take her wallet out of her smaller purse when she was switching bags.

"Why?"

"Luke, I forgot my wallet."

"No problem. I have money with me."

"That's not the point. I don't want to rely on you to pay for anything I might want to buy."

Tess was looking at him as she spoke, her voice sincere as she tried to make him understand that she preferred to pay her own way. It wasn't meant to insult him. He looked over at her, but the dark military aviator sunglasses he wore hid his eyes. It was hard to gauge his reaction, but he didn't appear to be offended.

"Understood. But since we're almost there it would be a waste of time to go back. Tell you what, we'll keep a running tab if you do buy anything, and you can pay me back when you get home."

She was pleased with the easy compromise he offered. "Deal, though I don't expect I'll be buying anything. I am there to work, after all." His only reply was a smile.

Moments later they rounded a corner, and Tess was immediately caught up in the scene in front of her. Luke stopped the cart, giving her time to take it all in. It was utterly delightful. Two roads were closed to all but foot traffic, and there was a ton of it, but no one seemed to be in any kind of a hurry to get from one cheerfully painted vendor's booth to the next. Beyond, the crystal-blue water of the sound beckoned invitingly in the mid-day sun. Sailboats dotted the glistening waves and sea-birds cried as they flew low overhead. She could hear laughter and music, a testament to the enjoyment of the crowd. The aromas drifting in the air were nothing short of blissful, causing her mouth to water in antici-pation of at least one bite of whatever smelled so entic-ing. She had thought the village was lovely when she arrived, but today it was dressed up for a party, which for her only added to its distinctive appeal.

"How could anyone ever want to leave here?" She spoke softly, wonder in each word.

"It's something else, isn't it?"

She heard the same appreciation in Luke's voice that she was feeling, and realized he felt the same way that she did about this special place.

"It's like Brigadoon. I'm afraid that if I close my eyes, it will disappear for a hundred years and I won't be able to find it again. I wonder if all of you know what you have."

"Oh, we know." He shifted in his seat to look at her as he spoke, his voice deep and low. "These folks nurture this place. It's a part of who they are. It's their home. They protect it and love it, and it gives back to them a hundred times over. The majority make their living from the sea out there. They're fishermen. It's been this way for a couple of centuries and hopefully will stay this way for a couple more. I'm proud to be a part of it."

Tess knew at that instant that she would have a difficult time leaving here when the time came to go. How could Livie have left? *Love.* Tess knew the answer before the thought had completely formed in her mind. Livie loved Adam so much that she was willing to be with him no matter where his career took him. Livie also knew that she always had this place to come back to. It was her foundation; it was in her soul. How could it not be? This town and its people had formed her values and helped shape her into the person they all loved so dearly.

Tess shook her head slightly, clearing her thoughts as she turned toward Luke, deeply aware of his arm lying casually behind her shoulders across the back of the seat.

"So, let's go join the party. I suspect that I'm not really helping out today." Tess smiled at Luke as she spoke.

"Nope. I knew you'd catch on. Your mission is to have fun, and my mission is to see that you do. When did you figure it out?" he asked curiously, as he drove down a small alleyway behind the vendors, pulling up near the church booth.

"When Aunt Annie called. I knew something was up. The aunts told me last night at dinner that they had a full roster of volunteers. She must have forgotten. What if I don't feel like having fun?"

"Are you upset?"

"Of course not. Luke, I—"

"Well, it's about time! What took you so long?" Katie interrupted as she made her way toward them, a smile lighting up her face.

"How's business? Looks like you sold quite a bit while I was gone." Luke had taken off his sunglasses and was eyeing the shelves behind the counter. "And it looks like you have plenty of help," he added, giving Tess a faint wink.

Katie didn't miss a beat as she cleared her throat a bit theatrically. "Oh, no, funny thing is we have plenty of help now, and will for the rest of the day. Sorry to have gotten you out for nothing, dear." Although she tried hard to look contrite, it just wasn't working.

Tess suppressed a smile. "That's all right. It's not as though I was busy with anything in particular." She leaned over and kissed the woman's weathered cheek as she assured her all was good. "Where's Aunt Annie?"

"Oh, she went off to carpe diem, as she calls it. I think she was headed in the direction of the shrimp burgers. She's been complaining about being hungry all day. I caught her eating some of the lemon cookies that Pastor Fulcher's wife made, and sent her to buy lunch for all of us. Who knows when or even if she'll come back."

"Since you don't need Tess, do you mind if I show her around?" Luke put his sunglasses back on as he spoke.

"Well, that of course is up to Tess, but it would be nice for her to see one of our little festivals in progress. Such a nice day for one." Katie adjusted her wide-brimmed hat as she spoke, throwing Luke a meaningful glance.

"I'd love to wander around for a bit, that is if Luke doesn't mind taking it a little slow. I'm afraid my leg isn't quite up to warp speed yet."

"Oh, my. I hadn't thought of your leg." This time Katie did look so sincerely contrite that Tess impulsively hugged her.

"I have thought of her leg," Luke assured the older woman. "We'll take frequent rest breaks. Nothing to it. Now, let's go seize the day!"

As they walked away Katie called, "Did you slather?"

"Yes!" both Tess and Luke answered at the same time.

"Good!"

Several hours later Tess found herself sitting on a wrought-iron bench under a Bradford pear tree in the town square, eating the most delicious mango shaved ice she had ever had. Well, technically it was the *only* mango shaved ice she had ever had, but what did that matter? The afternoon had been so much fun, everything about it was delicious. No bad thoughts or memories had intruded for the few hours they had been there, and Tess was grateful.

Luke had been as good as his word, taking frequent breaks to allow her to rest her leg. He wasn't obvious about it, but he did seem to instinctively know when she needed a seat for a short while. He never said a word, just guided her to a shady spot and joined her in people watching and small talk, seeming totally relaxed and content to be in her company.

Earlier, they'd made the rounds of the vendors and Tess had been impressed with the quality of the arts and crafts for sale, but she was most intrigued when they stopped by one of the jewelry booths. The artisan specialized in creating sea glass pieces that were absolutely stunning. Tess purchased five silver bangle bracelets inset with lovely frosted blue and green bits of glass. Two were for the aunts, and she planned on giving the other three to Livie and the girls. At first, she was not going to buy anything, but Luke encouraged her, agreeing that they were a bargain and that the ladies would love them. As he paid, Tess reminded him of their deal for her to reimburse him, and he didn't protest.

Then they stopped by the dunking booth to check on Caleb. He was having a great time with Joey and his dad. The minute Tess and Luke got there he ran up to them, a huge smile on his freckled face.

"Where have you been? Hey, Miss Tess! Dad, we need someone to dunk Mr. Joe really good!"

"Hi, buddy." Tess saw the love in Luke's eyes as he greeted the boy, then he glanced briefly at her, smiling. The tableau between father and son tugged at her heart and she smiled back without thinking.

"You do? Well, maybe I can help with that. Better yet, maybe Miss Tess would like to try."

Luke threw Tess a wink, but she was shaking her head.

"Oh, no. I really couldn't."

"Aw, c'mon, Miss Tess. I bet you could, if you really tried," Joey declared, coming to join them. Tess looked at all three males. Luke seemed as eager as the boys. She hated to disappoint them.

"Well, I did play a little softball in high school. Tell you what, how about if we both try. Luke?"

"Sounds good to me," he said with a crooked grin. "Have you had lunch?" he asked his son.

"Yep. Miss Linda bought us shrimp burgers. They sure were delicious!" Caleb looked so much like his father with his dark hair and beautiful blue eyes, Tess thought.

"Good deal. We need to get something to eat ourselves, and walk around for a while to enjoy the sights, but before the end of the day, we'll be back. Care to join us?

"Naw, they need my help here. Besides, I might miss someone dunking Mr. Joe. Promise you'll be back to try?"

"Promise."

"Roger that." Caleb snapped a smart salute and his dad returned it. "That's marine speak for okay," he explained to Joey as they ran back to the booth. Tess saw the boys salute each other, and laughed delightedly.

After they had visited Caleb, Luke had insisted on buying lunch for both of them and led her to a stall selling shrimp burgers. Tess's vision of chopped shrimp formed into a patty was nothing like the reality. Instead, the sandwich consisted of succulent whole fresh shrimp that were deep fried, placed on a toasted bun and covered with sweet and tangy coleslaw. She was ravenous and after the first bite wolfed the whole sandwich down in no time.

And now they sat in the town square, listening to a string quartet that had replaced the earlier band in the pavilion. The music was soft and classical, amplifying the serene perfection of a beautiful day. The sky was an amazing Carolina blue in color, with large, puffy white clouds gliding effortlessly through it. She could not remember having a better day for ages.

"Luke, where are you from?" She was curious. Certainly not from Swansboro, but she could not recall anyone having told her where he'd grown up.

For a long moment, he was silent. Her nervousness increased with every second that passed. Was this a touchy subject for him? Tess started to open her mouth to retract the question and change the subject, but stopped herself before the words could come out. Maybe, like her, he needed to talk about the things that had hurt him in the past. Maybe in this, she could be there for him as he had been for her.

He looked at Tess thoughtfully. He wondered how much he should say. It had been a complicated childhood for him, with one parent totally absent and the other struggling with a substance abuse problem. He'd spent it moving from one foster home to the next, until he had landed in a considerable amount of trouble. Part of him was ashamed to admit how much of a mess his childhood had been.

Then he realized it didn't matter. He had nothing to hide, and his life since joining the Corps was so different than it had been while growing up. Mentally, Luke amended that thought. His life since he had let God in was now vastly different. That, coupled with the discipline he had gained while in the Marine Corps, had made him a person he was proud to be—a person who could handle the amazing responsibility he'd been given in the form of his son.

"I'm from a small town in East Tennessee called Greenville. Beautiful place."

"Is your family still there?"

Luke noticed that Tess had shifted her position on the bench to face him, taking off her sunglasses and putting them in her bag, which sat between them. Her eyes studied him with interest.

"My sister lives there. She and her husband have a farm in the area. They have six great kids that I love dearly."

"Six? Wow! A nice big family. How often do you get to see them?"

Luke relaxed against the back of the bench, stretching his legs out in front of him.

"Not as often as I'd like," he admitted ruefully. "Caleb and I were just there last month. I took him to see his grandparents—his mother's parents. Before that, it had been a long time. I'm working on changing that, though. Life is far too short to not be with the people that love you and who you love most."

"I agree. I would hate not seeing my family often. Although my parents are in Africa right now. I haven't seen them since…" She faltered, furrowing her brow. "Well, since they came home when I got hurt."

"Africa? What are they doing there?"

"Dad is a doctor with Hope Corps, the organization I volunteered for when I was sent to Afghanistan. Mom works with him. She's a nurse practitioner. And of course, you know Livie and Adam and the girls. But what about you? Your parents?"

He had tried to turn the conversation back to her, without success. He knew she wasn't being pushy, just curious to know about him, who he was and where he came from. His childhood was no big secret. He often shared it with the kids he mentored at the youth center. He wanted to let them know that he understood where they were coming from, their problems and what they had to deal with. But telling Tess was different. For some reason he felt a little uneasy about sharing this side of him with her. He rubbed the back of his neck before answering.

"I have no idea where my father is. I haven't seen him since he left. I was four years old. My mother, I do see occasionally, when I visit home. She didn't raise me. After Dad left she started drinking, heavily. She was physically and emotionally abusive to my sister and me. We were eventually removed from her home and put into foster care."

"That makes for a pretty tough childhood. No kid should have to go through that."

Luke shot her a quick glance after she spoke. In her eyes he saw concern, compassion and kindness for the little boy he had been and what he'd gone through.

"I was an angry kid for a long time," he admitted, choosing his words carefully.

It still stung when he thought back on the times his mother, in a drunken rage, had screamed that she wished he had never been born. That his father would never have left if she hadn't had children. It was then that Luke had learned how cruel words, especially from someone that you loved, had the ability to cut deeply, causing substantial pain. He had loved his mother unconditionally and still did. When she was sober, she was loving and kind. Problem was, she hadn't been sober that often during his childhood, at least not when he was around her. Hopefully, this new stint in rehab was helping her. He prayed that it did.

"I am so very sorry that you had to go through that. Some people were never meant to be parents. It's always tragic for the kids involved."

Tess's tone was soothing. She reached over and lightly rubbed his shoulder as she spoke, tenderness and understanding lacing each softly spoken word. Her touch felt right, too right. He pulled back slightly, not wanting to offend her, yet needing to put some distance between them. He had the most insane urge to kiss her right now, and he doubted very much she would appreciate it. Gruffly, he cleared his throat before going on.

"So, here I am, years later, and none the worse for wear."

"Yes, here you are and probably a *bit* worse for wear. How could you not be?"

"Thank you, Tess."

"For what?" She looked a little confused.

"For listening. I appreciate that."

"Oh. Well, you're welcome, then." She gave him a little smile. Abruptly, he jumped to his feet, extending his hand to her.

"Come on. We have one more booth to hit and then home."

"Oh, that's right. The dunking booth!" Tess laughed as she tossed what was left of her shaved ice in the trash bin and took Luke's outstretched hand.

"We promised the boys we'd dunk Joe. The poor kids have probably been trying to do it themselves for the past couple of hours. You did tell them you played softball in high school. They're expecting big things from you."

Tess shook her head. "Maybe you should try, Luke. High school softball was a while ago for me."

"Oh, no, Tess. It's all on you."

Her only response was to make a face at him, crinkling her pert nose.

The dunking booth was only a short walk away. Caleb and Joey were standing at the counter with two other boys. Caleb's face lit up when he saw them approaching, and he waved them over excitedly. Luke's heart warmed. He didn't know what tomorrow would bring, but today was good, and the good days were adding up. It had been tough getting used to each other. He was trying hard to be the best father he could be. He knew it would never be perfect between them; it never was, between parent and child. Building a loving relationship took hard work, especially since he and Caleb had known each other only six months.

One day at a time, Luke reminded himself. Baby steps.

"Over here, Miss Tess, Dad!"

"Has anyone dunked him yet? Hi, Mark, Kevin."

Tess watched Luke ruffle his son's dark hair and then

wave to Joe, who was perched on a plank suspended above a tank of water, kicking his legs back and forth. He wore an old-fashioned one-piece striped bathing suit that looked ridiculously appropriate.

Joe waved back, giving them a broad grin. "Come to give it a try, Luke?" he taunted.

"Not me," Luke replied, pointing to Tess at his side.

"Only five people got him in the water. I was hoping for more." Joey looked more than a little disappointed as he recited the numbers. "But Dad says we made a lot of money for the clinic."

"That's the important thing, Joey. Well, let's see what Miss Tess can do, shall we?" Luke put several dollars on the counter and Joey handed them three softballs.

"Aim for that flat round thing," Caleb instructed Tess as she handed her cane to Luke and picked up the first ball. "You just gotta win the big prize. We don't wanna give it to anyone else."

"I'll do my best. What's the big prize?"

"A puppy."

"Puppy?" She looked over at Luke, one brow raised.

Luke pointed to the shelves of stuffed animals behind the counter, including several dogs in pastel hues. She gave a relieved nod and smiled gamely at the boys as she positioned herself in front of the tank, tossing the ball in the air and catching it a few times while eyeing the police chief, who had begun to heckle her.

"Come on, Tess, give it your best shot. I bet you couldn't hit the broad side of a barn." He was clearly enjoying himself.

"Probably not," she agreed serenely, unaware of

the small crowd that had gathered behind her until she heard appreciative laughter.

She almost froze then, suddenly shy in front of so many people. She knew she wouldn't be graceful, with her leg still giving her problems. Now, she just wanted to go back to the cottage. Stupid of her to think she could get through even part of a day without the old insecurities and issues rearing their ugly heads. *Fight through it*, she ordered herself sternly. She forced herself to wind up and release the ball.

Her first throw missed the mark by a wide distance. A collective groan issued from the peanut gallery as they vocally commiserated with her. She bit her lip and looked over at Joey and Caleb. She didn't want to let them down.

The little boys just shook their heads before smiling at her encouragingly and giving her a thumbs-up. *Oh, to have the blind faith of a child*, she thought.

"Aw, she can't do it," one of the other boys said, looking at Caleb with disgust.

"Yes, she can. First ones don't count," he declared. "You got this, Miss Tess. Shake it off."

"Oh, I'm so scared. That was too close for comfort!" Joe chortled gleefully from his perch, egging her on as she picked up the second ball and weighed it carefully in her hand. Unfortunately for the chief, his next words sealed his fate. "Come on! You throw like a girl. A girlie girl!"

"I am a girl," Tess affirmed with quiet confidence, then mentally blocked out everything and everyone around her, concentrating at the target just past the laughing man sitting smugly above the water-filled tank.

In her mind's eye she visualized herself on the pitcher's mound in the state play-offs fifteen years earlier. The release lever became the snug pit of Ally Gleason's catcher's mitt as Tess wound up and quickly discharged the ball in one smooth, underhand motion, taking dead aim at her target. The ball traveled with such speed and force that it bent the lever on the booth as Joe went feet first into the water, an incredulous look on his face. She heard a loud whoop from Joey and Caleb, and appreciative applause from the group around the booth as she found herself being lifted in Luke's strong arms.

"Good girl!" His laughing eyes locked with hers before he kissed her soundly on the cheek. Then she was on the ground again, feeling more than a little unsteady. Her cheeks flushed, and she reached instinctively for her cane as the boys rushed to join them.

She could have imagined that kiss on the cheek, it had happened so quickly. *Had* she imagined it? She peeked at Luke from under her lashes, but his face gave nothing away. Evidently, it hadn't affected him as it had her. He looked perfectly relaxed, as if nothing out of the ordinary had happened. Tess felt a small stab of irritation with herself for her reaction, and with him for his nonreaction, then pushed it away. It was only a congratulatory peck on the cheek, nothing more. He was probably used to casually kissing all sorts of women for all sorts of reasons.

"Here's the prize, Miss Tess. Her name is Jackie O, but I call her Jack."

"Jack?" Tess asked faintly, looking down at Joey as he shoved a small white wiggling bundle of fluff into her arms.

"Yeah. Our dogs Bogey and Bacall had puppies and Jack is the last one left."

"Joey, this is a real puppy." Tess pointed out the obvious.

"Cool, huh? We had the best grand prizes in the whole festival. Mom wanted to sell the puppies, but I talked her into giving them to the winners. Well, if they wanted one. 'Course, not everyone did. Can't figure out why not. Who wouldn't want a puppy?"

Tess's gaze traveled from the earnest face of the ten-year-old standing in front of her to the fuzzy white face of the small dog in her arms and back again. How could she say no? She suddenly became aware of the small group around them watching the scene with avid interest. The puppy chose that moment to lick her hand and wag her curly little tail as she stared up at Tess with brown button eyes. Tess knew she was lost.

"I can't imagine who wouldn't want a puppy, Joey. It *is* the best prize ever."

"I told you guys she was the coolest girl." Joey looked at his friends, who were in turn looking at Tess with a mixture of awe and respect. "She even likes turtles and snakes."

Luke put his arm casually around Tess's shoulders and gave her a small squeeze of approval before pointing out that she would need to get a few things for the puppy before going home.

"We've got you covered on that." Joe had joined them,

towel in hand, grinning from ear to ear. "There's a sack of puppy chow and a small bed behind the counter. Sure you want the puppy, Tess? Don't let Joey bully you into it. And where in the world did you learn to throw like that, girl?"

Tess started to answer, but was cut off by another voice.

"Yes, Tess. Do tell. Where did you learn to throw like that? And you, Luke. You've been showing her around? More of those random acts of kindness you're so fond of?"

Sarah Fulcher's voice was pleasant, but one look at her and Tess knew the woman was feeling anything but kindly. Her violet eyes were flashing fire as she glanced from Luke to Tess and back again. Tess noticed the small crowd was watching them avidly. *Time to go home*, she thought, hugging the puppy a little closer. She was abruptly very tired. Her leg was aching and the last thing she wanted was to be the center of more attention.

"Hi, Sarah. Nope, not me being kind. Tess is being kind in taking the puppy." Luke didn't miss a beat, a genuine smile on his face as he spoke to the other woman.

Sarah looked doubtful for a minute and then turned a charming smile on Tess. "How generous of you. It's a cute little thing, isn't it?"

"I didn't adopt her. I won her. And she is cute." Tess couldn't keep the abruptness out of her voice. Turning to Luke, she added, "I really need to go home now." It wasn't a question, it was a statement.

He must have seen the strain in her eyes because he didn't say a word, just nodded and went to collect Caleb.

"Luke, I need to speak with you about something when you have a minute," Sarah called out to him.

"I'll phone you later, Sarah. Right now I want to get Tess home."

Sarah hesitated, then said, "Of course," and walked away, her high heels clicking loudly on the pavement.

Chapter Seven

The air was thick with humidity as Luke put the truck in gear and left the parking lot of base legal. Dark clouds were building to the east and he heard the menacing rumble of thunder in the distance. A storm was brewing. It suited his mood today.

The packet that contained the newly changed legal documents was sitting on the seat next to him. He had changed his will, making Caleb the beneficiary. He had also made Jen's parents Caleb's guardians in the event that anything should happen to him. Those had been easy decisions. It was the threat of them taking Caleb from him in the near future that had Luke worried. The lawyer had advised him that there was nothing he could do except wait, something he was not very good at doing. The lawyer was researching the laws in Tennessee and would get back to him. The best thing Luke could do for now was to make sure that he had a stable, healthy, happy home for his son, which he was trying very hard to do.

There was still the issue of adequate child care. He had thought hard about asking Tess, as the sisters had suggested, but he balked at the idea. She had enough on her plate with working through her PTSD issues. A kid running around wouldn't be any help. But it was coming down to the wire and he had to do something. He was interviewing another candidate this afternoon. He prayed that this one would be it. He needed to get home, pick up Caleb from the Masons' house and get ready for the interview.

His thoughts turned to Tess again. It had been five days since he had seen her at the festival last Saturday. She had been conspicuously absent from church services on Sunday. Whether she was deliberately avoiding people or her faith was still in question in her mind, he had no idea. It could be a combination of the two. For his part, he was certain that her faith in God had never left her, but she was too angry to forgive Him for what had happened. Only God could help her with that, and Luke had no doubt that He would.

The fact of the matter was that he wanted to see how she was getting on. He was concerned about her but didn't want to be pushy. Still, it might not be a bad idea to check on her. He made a mental note to call her later this afternoon, but first things first. The nanny.

His jaw was set with determination as he pulled into the neat, hedge-lined driveway of the Mason house. Large raindrops began to spatter forcefully on his windshield as lightning flashed overhead and thunder boomed loudly all around him. The storm had started, but it was nothing compared to the one raging inside him. He had to make this interview work, for his sake as well as Caleb's.

Linda met him at the front entrance, ushering him inside and out of the elements. "Come in, come in." She closed the door and faced him with a grin. "The boys are playing in the bedroom. I'll get Caleb. Want a cup of coffee?"

"No, I'm good," Luke called after her departing figure. It didn't take the boys long to hit the living room with an almost supersonic burst of energy.

"Hi, Dad!" Caleb came to sit on the sofa next to him, an eager look on his young face.

"Hi, buddy. Have a good day?"

"Yep! Can I camp out with Joey tonight?"

"Can he, Mr. Luke?" Joey asked, plopping down on Luke's other side.

Before he could say yes or no, Caleb jumped in again excitedly. "It's for our camping merit badge for Scouts. Mr. Joe said he'd help us."

Luke looked at Linda for guidance.

"It's true. They're going to camp in the backyard. Tent's already up and the fire pit has a stockpile of wood under a tarp. Joe wanted to know if you'd like to join them, if Caleb can stay. Didn't quite count on the rain, though. Hope the lightning subsides." Linda didn't look too concerned about the weather as she glanced out the window at the raging storm. A loud clap of thunder made them all jump a little, however.

"Well, that sounded close," she admitted, before turning back to Luke.

"I don't see why not. In fact, I'd like to go camping

with the boys and Joe. Great idea! But I have an interview for the nanny position in—" His words were cut short by the ringing of a cell phone. It wasn't his; he had left it in the car.

"Not mine. It's in my purse." Linda was looking around the room. "Maybe Joe left his?" She had a puzzled look on her face as the phone kept ringing insistently. "No, he called about an hour ago, so he has his with him." She had gotten up and was searching the room, trying to locate the phone, when it stopped. Then it started again. It was at that moment that Luke looked down at his son. He saw the stricken look on the boy's face and realized the sound was emanating from the vicinity of his leg. Caleb had a cell phone? Caleb had a cell phone!

"Hand it over," Luke said, as the boy tried to inch his way off the sofa. Luke put a hand on his arm to stop him, holding out his other palm. Caleb hesitated, then heaved a defeated sigh as he reached in his pocket and handed over the phone, his eyes fixed on the floor.

"Where did you get this, Caleb?" Luke asked gently.

"Grampy gave it to me." His eyes were still fixed on the carpeted floor.

"Look at me, Caleb, please. Why didn't you tell me?"

"Grampy said not to ever tell you because you would take it away and I wouldn't be able to talk to him then." The words came out in a rush, and Luke's heart broke at the hurt look on his son's face. But this was wrong on a couple of levels and he needed Caleb to understand that. "And you did take it away and now I can't talk to Grampy when he calls me."

"Caleb, have I ever tried to stop you from calling your grandparents?"

Luke pulled Caleb closer as he spoke, draping an arm around his shoulders. He felt the boy stiffen and try to pull away, but Luke wouldn't allow it. There was a problem here and he needed to get to the bottom of it. Out of the corner of his eye, he saw Linda usher Joey out of the room.

"No, sir." Caleb's voice was low and he sounded on the verge of tears.

"And I never would. I told you, you can call them whenever you want to and we'll go to Nashville to see them a lot. I want you to be in touch with them. I know they love you and you love them. Family is important." Luke kept his voice gentle as he spoke, trying desperately to make his son understand. "But being honest with each other is important, too. And that means not hiding things like this from me. Grampy should have asked me before he gave the phone to you. That was wrong."

"But he couldn't ask you, Dad. He couldn't."

"Why not?" Luke was trying to follow what Caleb was saying, but it didn't make sense.

"Because you weren't there. I mean, he gave me the phone last year, when Mom was with me. He told me not to tell her, either, because she would take it away from me, too."

Caleb looked absolutely miserable by this point and Luke was at a loss. Why would Dave Lockard have felt Caleb should have a secret phone to hide from his mother? They needed to sort this out, but for now Luke put the phone in his pocket.

"We'll work this out, son. It will be okay. I'll talk to Grampy."

"Are you mad at me again, Dad?"

Luke was caught off guard by the question. Mad? Again? "Of course not, Caleb. And why did you say *again*?"

"You were mad at me when I went to the island with Joey," the boy reminded him.

"Ah, I see. Yes, I was angry," Luke admitted. "And I was scared. You could have been hurt and I would have had no way of knowing where you were or that you needed my help. You have to understand that you can't just take a boat out on the open water when you don't know what you're doing. We have rules for a reason. They keep you safe and make you a better person when it's time for you to go out in the world. Rules help teach life's lessons. Do you understand?"

Caleb nodded, hesitating before he spoke. "Can I have the phone back?"

Luke shook his head. "No, you can't. Sorry, buddy, but you're too young to have a cell phone."

"But Grampy will be mad at me." The boy looked so close to tears that Luke almost gave in, but he held fast. He knew that consistency was important with a child.

"I'll deal with Grampy. Don't you worry about it. It's over. Got it?"

"Got it." Caleb was obviously not happy, given the deep frown on his face, but at least he wasn't arguing.

"I'm sorry, son, but that's the way it is. We'll talk about it when you get a little older."

"I might not be here when I'm older."

"Why do you say that, Caleb?" Luke was taken aback. Surely the boy didn't know about the custody issues. Had his grandparents been talking to him about going back to Tennessee? Luke looked at him closely. What was going on in that young mind?

"You might not want me to stay with you because sometimes I'm not nice to you. Or you could die. Mom did."

"I see. You're afraid that I might die, too? So you don't want to get too attached to me."

Caleb nodded, and Luke saw the pain and uncertainty in the boy's eyes. He could only imagine how frightened and bewildered he must be after everything that had happened to him in the past year.

Luke had made certain that he found someone on base that both he and Caleb could talk to, a therapist that could help them navigate the shoals and eddies that their new circumstances were bound to create, had created. But just now he was wondering how to reassure a child who had already lost one parent that everything would be okay? This problem had never come up in their sessions. Luke felt his heart swell with overwhelming compassion and love for his son as Caleb stared intently at the carpet.

Luke was a combat-tested marine who had just discovered his Achilles' heel. His boy. Caleb's pain was his pain right now, and somehow, he had to make things better for him. Somehow he had to come up with the right words, and so he prayed hard to find them. He took a deep breath before he spoke.

"Caleb, your mother and God have tasked me with the most important mission of my life: taking care of you. They both have faith that I can do it. I believe that I can, too. But I can't do it without your help. I need for you to meet me halfway. I need you to believe that I can do it—that I'll be here for you no matter what."

He stopped then, gauging Caleb's reaction to his words, but the boy's face was shuttered. Luke couldn't tell what he was thinking, so he continued. "As for me dying and going to be with God, we will all die someday, son. It's God's plan for us. I hate that your mom died, but she is with God. And just for the record, I plan to be around for a long time."

"Grampy is mad at God for taking Mom away."

Luke shook his head. "Caleb, God is all-loving. Don't ever be angry with Him, like your Grampy is." *Like Tess is, as well,* he thought fleetingly. "He loves you, just like I do. It's a special love. A love like no other." Luke paused, again searching for words that would comfort the child. But he didn't have to look for them long; they came quickly, and he knew they were right, as surely as he knew the sun would set that evening and rise again the next morning. *Thank You, Lord,* he prayed silently.

"As for not wanting you to stay here with me, I will always want you. Always. You are my son and I love you unconditionally. Do you know what that means?"

"No." The kid looked positively miserable, and Luke's first instinct was to hug him, but he held back.

"Look at me, Caleb, not the floor." Luke put a gentle finger under Caleb's chin and lifted it until he was looking into his son's blue eyes. "It means that there are no limits on my love for you. I don't stop loving you because sometimes you may have a bad day and might not be the nicest kid on the block." Luke took a deep breath before continuing, "I know you get homesick and I know you miss your mom. I know coming to live with me and moving to a new place has been hard for you. You're allowed to have bad moments, but when you do, and you want to talk, I'm always here for you. Always."

"Okay." Caleb still didn't seem convinced, but there was a thoughtful look on his face as he digested the words. Luke hoped that he had gotten through to him. He had had no idea that the boy was afraid to get close because he was fearful of losing him, too. It explained so much.

"Now, we have a nanny to interview. Go thank Miss Linda and tell her that we'll be back for the campout a little later."

"Yes, sir." Caleb shot him a tentative smile before going to the kitchen to find Linda.

An hour later, Luke closed his front door and shook his head. Another no. Highly educated, with impeccable references, the woman had seemed perfect until the end of the interview, when she had asked to see her room. Luke explained that it wasn't a live-in position and she had cut the interview short.

Tiredly, he rubbed the back of his neck. His options had run out. He had no idea what he was going to do now. *Tess*, an inner voice reminded him, but he dismissed it as quickly as he heard it.

"That's okay, Dad, I didn't like her, anyway. Besides, we couldn't give her Mike's room. I mean, he needs a place to sleep when he gets home."

Luke knew that Caleb was trying to make the best of another nanny candidate gone south. Still, it was true that his roommate and fellow marine, Mike Forrester, wouldn't be happy if his bed was taken when he got back from Afghanistan.

He had not met Caleb personally yet, but the two had met via Skype and Mike seemed to have a way with the kid. They had liked each other right away and it was good to see Caleb talking to the other man a mile a minute, asking questions about the country and people—and about Mike himself and his job in the Marine Corps.

His friend was an invaluable sounding board, and Luke was grateful for the technology that allowed them to stay connected. Mike had been with Luke via Skype and phone from the minute he had gotten Caleb, serving as a major source of support and encouragement over the past six months. In fact, he had been able to talk to his buddy for about an hour after the fair last Saturday and Mike's sensible advice about the situation with Caleb's grandparents had helped center Luke once again.

It was good to have an anchor, someone who was on his side, someone whom he had known for years. Mike's deployment in the war-torn country would end soon, as his year was almost up, and he would be making his way home. Luke was looking forward to introducing his son to his best friend face-to-face.

"No, son, we can't give Mike's room away."

Tess. Again his inner voice nudged him in her direction. She was going through a tough time, but as Katie and Annie had pointed out, perhaps Caleb was what she needed to help pull her through it. Luke felt that God had brought her back into his life for a reason. Maybe this was it. Besides which, he was stuck between a rock and a hard place right now. He didn't want to place the boy in day care, especially as they were still getting to know each other. He felt in his heart that it was important to have Caleb in a home environment for now. Maybe next year he would consider it, or a day camp, but not yet. He made up his mind to speak to her, if Caleb was on board with the idea.

"Caleb, what do you think of Miss Tess?"

"Now, her, I like." The answer was immediate.

"How about as a nanny?" Luke wanted to be certain how his son felt about her as a caretaker before he spoke to her.

"Yes!" Caleb nodded his head emphatically. "Are you gonna ask her, Dad?"

"Yes, I think I am. Go pack your overnight bag and I'll run you over to Joey's house."

Tess leaned down and picked up Jack, settling the puppy comfortably on her lap before reaching for her headphones. She didn't want to hear the thunder as the storm broke. With soothing classical music playing in her ears, she could almost ignore the loud cracks and booms. She could pretend they didn't remind her of the explosions of artillery that had destroyed the orphanage and so many lives on that awful day.

She'd always loved thunderstorms until the bombing. She smiled softly as the calming strains of Twelve Fantasias for Violin worked on her nerves, lulling her into a peaceful place far away from painful memories. Absently, she stroked Jack's soft white fur as the puppy gave a small, contented sigh and drifted into sleep, nestled in the safe haven of her lap.

Good idea, she thought. It was a lovely rainy afternoon, the best time for a short nap. With the thunder only a distant rumble, muffled by the headphones and soothing music, Tess closed her eyes and slipped into a gentle sleep where she surprisingly dreamed of nothing.

"Tess, wake up. Come on, honey, wake up."

Terms of endearment. That really is so nice, Tess thought as she drifted in that peaceful place between asleep and awake. *Funny, it sounded like Luke.*

"Tess, I need to speak to you."

His voice was low and gentle, but there was a sense of urgency that caught at Tess. Something was wrong. She needed to wake up. She fought through layers of limbo, opening her eyes slowly to find him crouched next to the chair, the headphones in one hand and a tender smile softening the hard lines of his face. Still half-asleep, she returned the smile, not thinking it odd that he should be in the cottage. In fact, it seemed right for him to be there.

"Hey," she murmured quietly.

"Hey back."

He reached out as he spoke, gently brushing her cheek with the back of his strong hand. She closed her eyes for a moment at the tender gesture, then realization hit her like a brick. Her eyes flew open and she sat straight up in the chair, almost knocking poor Jack to the floor. The puppy gave a small yip in response.

"Luke! What are you doing here? Is everything all right? What time is it?"

"I'm really sorry to have let myself in, but I knocked a few times and you didn't hear me. I saw you through the front window. I didn't realize you were sleeping. I thought you just couldn't hear because of the headphones." She saw the apology in his eyes and shook her head.

"No, no. It's fine. Really. I didn't want to hear the thunder, so I put music on and…" Her voice trailed away as she worried that the explanation sounded lame.

He reached for her hand, empathy etched on every line of his face. "I get it. Clever girl," he said approvingly. "The thunder reminds you of live fire and makes you a little jumpy."

She nodded, grateful as always for his understanding. "It's getting better. Really it is." She didn't know whether she was trying to convince herself or him, but regardless, it was more than nice to have someone who understood her motives so precisely.

"Of course it is. And it will keep on getting better. I promise."

His voice had a soothing quality that played on her senses like a blessed hymn. There was something so familiar about it, and again she had that nagging feeling that she had heard it before somewhere.

"Speaking from experience?" she asked with a half smile.

"Way too much," he confirmed, leaning back on his heels and rubbing the back of his neck.

"Luke, what's wrong?"

She was becoming concerned. He would never just walk into her house this way and wake her for casual conversation. He would have come back another time if whatever he needed to discuss with her wasn't urgent. She studied him closely. His eyes had a tired, haunted look that he could not have disguised if he tried.

"Tess, I really need your help with something. I wouldn't ask if it weren't so important."

"I'll help if I can." It was the look of pure exhaustion on his face that made her speak without thinking. Without saying another word she gently put Jack on the floor, got up and took Luke's hand, leading him to the kitchen and settling him at the old pine table.

Chapter Eight

"Have you eaten today?" she asked as she began brewing a pot of coffee.

"Not that I can recall," he admitted with a shake of his head. "I haven't really had time."

"Join me for dinner?"

She already had the fixings out of the refrigerator for grilled cheese sandwiches, and was pouring homemade vegetable soup into a pan on the stove. He would talk when he was ready, and in the meantime, hopefully, the comfort food would help soothe his psyche.

"I'd like that."

"Good. I hate eating alone. Plus I have a meeting this evening that I promised the aunts I would attend, so I need to eat before going."

"So do I—hate eating alone, that is. You're going to a meeting?"

She nodded as she put a pat of butter in the frying pan. "I told them I'd drive them because of the weather.

Not that I have a clue as to what the meeting is about, mind you."

"You're one of God's good souls, Tess Greenwood."

Tess felt her cheeks warm at the gentle praise, and turned quickly toward the stove so that Luke couldn't see her blush.

"I don't know about that," she muttered quietly. "He and I are still having issues over what happened the day I got hurt. I can't get past the fact that He would let so many children die."

"I do know you are a good soul. And what happened that day was part of His plan. You need to accept that, come to terms with it." Luke had come up behind her and put his hands on her shoulders. Turning her to face him, he looked intently into her eyes.

"You're saying things that I know in my head," Tess admitted. "But my heart still aches."

"Of course it does, but you can't hang on to that particular heartache forever. It does you no earthly good, not if you're intent on going forward. You'll always have heartaches in your life. The trick is not to hold on to them. Grieve, let them go and steel yourself for the next, because it will surely come. It's called living. Life is not full of trials, but they exist as surely as every joyful thing that God gives us."

Tess looked at Luke, slightly in awe. His take on life was amazing, particularly in light of the childhood he had told her about, not to mention the curveball fate had thrown him with Caleb.

"You know, Luke, *you* are truly one of God's good souls. And just for the record, I'm making progress, thanks in large part to you." Suddenly she felt shy, so she shooed him over to the table and changed the subject.

"Hungry?"

"Starved!"

That slow, confounding smile she had come to know so well played around his mouth, crinkling the corners of his beautiful eyes as he took his seat again. In no time she had the table set with two steaming bowls of fragrant soup, and had whipped up a couple grilled cheese sandwiches, artisan bread crunchy on the outside, with delicious hot and creamy Gruyère centers. She served Luke and took a seat opposite him at the table.

They ate in companionable silence, the rain softly tapping on the copper roof, providing a pleasant background for the impromptu meal. Thankfully, the thunder had stopped.

It was gratifying to her to watch him enjoy what she had prepared with so little effort. She was a nester and nurturer at heart and rarely had the opportunity to cook for someone other than herself.

At the end of the meal, he pushed his bowl and plate away with a satisfied sigh. "That was delicious. You're quite a chef. Homemade soup?"

"Is there any other kind?" Tess arched a brow in response, causing him to laugh.

"Not in your world, I take it?"

"Never. My mother would kill me if she ever found a can of soup in my kitchen. Besides, it's so easy to make and much better for you than that canned garbage. I'm really glad you liked it." Tess collected the dishes as she spoke, putting them in the sink, and brought two cups of coffee back to the table. Seeing that he seemed to be feeling better, she broached the subject that had been on her mind since he had awakened her.

"Luke, why did you come over? You said you had to speak to me about something. Are you all right?" She couldn't keep the concern out of her voice, although she tried. She watched him closely as he took a sip of coffee before answering.

"I need your help."

"I'll help you in any way that I can." She didn't hesitate to offer again.

"I'm glad to hear you say that." The relief on his ruggedly handsome face was obvious, and a small warning bell sounded inside Tess. This was serious, whatever it was.

"Now you're scaring me."

"No, no. It's nothing to be afraid of. Maybe I'm doing this all wrong, I don't know." He looked uncertain for a fleeting second and then his visage took on its normal, composed expression. Yet he stayed silent. It was as if he couldn't seem to find the words.

"Whatever it is, I'll help you deal with it, if I can." She doubted that he was deliberately dragging this out, but it seemed to be taking forever for him to speak.

"Tess, would you be willing to take care of Caleb during the day while I'm at work?"

Tess was more than a little surprised by the request. Of course she couldn't do it. He must be desperate to even ask her. He held up a hand when she tried to speak.

"Please, hear me out before giving me an answer.

Linda Mason normally takes care of him, but she starts a new job on Monday and won't be able to any longer. I've interviewed at least ten people to take the position, but for one reason or another, none of them panned out."

Again, Tess saw the exhaustion etched on his handsome face. If only she *could* help him. But it was impossible. She couldn't take on a child while she was still struggling to take care of herself.

"Surely there are better people than me to handle this for you. People you know and love. People you trust. We barely know each other. Besides, I have Jack to take care of. I can't leave her alone all day. I'm training her."

Luke gave a shake his head. "It's no good. I love and trust the Salter sisters, but they're too old to take care of a ten-year-old boy. He'd run them ragged in a heartbeat. And everyone else I can think of has work of their own that they need to do during the day. I could bring him here in the mornings, so you wouldn't have to leave Jack alone." Luke paused as if weighing his next words carefully. "Tess, if I can't get a nanny for him, I'm afraid he may be taken away from me." He spoke in a low voice, his face almost blank; except for the pain in his eyes.

"What do you mean?"

"His grandparents want custody of him. I'm afraid that anything they can find to use against me, they will. If you'd consent to do this for me, I'd be grateful."

His words chased through her mind at incredible speed. Tess knew Luke was afraid. He had to be. The mere thought of losing his son had to be terrifying. She hated to say no. She knew instinctively that he was a man who rarely asked for help with anything. He was so self-sufficient and competent. This couldn't be easy for him. Perhaps there was a compromise. Maybe she could take Caleb just until Luke found someone better qualified.

"All right, Luke. I'll do it, but only until you can find a person better suited to Caleb's and your needs. I'm not the answer to your problem, but I can buy you time." She reached out a hand and covered his large one, giving it a strong squeeze.

The relief on his face was tangible. "Thank you, Tess. Thank you." He breathed the words almost like a prayer of gratitude.

"Are you sure you want me to do this? That you trust me with your son?" She couldn't keep the doubt out of her voice.

"I'm positive. I trust you implicitly. There really is no one else that I can think of that I want to do this. I appreciate you helping me."

She stood and picked up the puppy, needing something soft and warm to hold on to right about now.

"From your lips to God's ears," she murmured softly.

"Are *you* certain you can do this, Tess? Do you feel uneasy?"

She caught the look of concern on his face. Evidently, he had just realized that she might be unsure of herself.

"I believe that I can help you. And I will do my best for your son." She was sincere as she gazed back at him, masking her concern with a smile.

Tess hugged the puppy close. Luke really did look uncertain now. Was it a trick of the soft light in the kitchen? She doubted that Luke Barrett had many uncertain moments in his life. Then his face cleared and he smiled broadly.

"You know, Tess, I believe that you just might be the perfect choice of nanny for my son. I think this is God's will at work."

"I doubt that, but believe what you like," she muttered. If it was God's will, once again, God was wrong. She refrained from voicing her opinion out loud, though, just glad to see the smile on Luke's face and hear the relief in his voice.

She got up from the table and walked over to the French doors that opened out on the garden and the sound beyond. The water was anything but calm this afternoon, mirroring her own mixed emotions. Lightning arced across the horizon, trailing down to touch the rough surface of the sea in the distance. It was beautiful and powerful.

Luke came up behind her, putting his hands on her shoulders and leaning down to kiss the top of her head. "Thank you, Tess. You've helped me more than you know."

His words were so heartfelt that she was left in no doubt that she had done the right thing—for him. As for herself, she was not sure at all.

"Just remember, you have to find a replacement as soon as possible." She hadn't meant the words to sound hard, but they did.

Tess pulled away and walked over to the sink to get a glass of water. Her throat was suddenly dry as the reality of the situation sank in. She had just agreed to watch a ten-year-old boy. She must be out of her mind.

She watched Luke rub the back of his neck again before he spoke. "I wish we had more time to give you to think about it. I really do. But I don't have that luxury to offer you, or me."

Tess was rather proud of her sensible reply. "No worries, Luke. It's only a temporary arrangement. You'll find a replacement as soon as possible. It will work out."

"Right," he confirmed with a nod. She was a little taken aback by the speed with which he agreed.

"Right." She gave a vigorous nod in return, then thought of the hour. "Oh, my, what time is it?"

"A little after six. Why?"

"I promised the aunts I'd drive them to that meeting. I'm sorry, Luke, but I have to get ready or I'll be late. The meeting is at six thirty." She had almost forgotten, with everything else that had gone on. She couldn't let the aunts down. Tess felt panicky as she rose to her feet and looked around for her cane, then remembered it was in the living room.

"Relax. You have plenty of time. I have to get going, too. Caleb and Joey are camping out tonight in the backyard with Joe and me."

"In this weather?" Tess asked as she glanced out the window again. "Doesn't look like it's going to let up anytime soon."

"I know what you mean, but I somehow doubt it will matter to the boys."

Tess laughed. "You're probably right." Then a thought occurred to her. "When do I start with Caleb?"

"Bright and early Monday morning, if that's okay?"

"Fine. Are you sure you don't mind him coming here?"

"Not at all. I'll make a list of incidentals, including important phone numbers and medical information, his food likes and dislikes. He also has Scouts once a week and football camp is coming up. It'll be late in the day so I should be able to get him there myself, but do you mind taking him if I'm late arriving home? I'll buy groceries for you, and you never asked about salary."

Tess was surprised when he mentioned money. "I assumed I was doing it as a favor. No money involved. And I don't mind taking him where he needs to go." She had honestly not given it a thought.

"Of course you'll be paid." Luke's voice was firm as he mentioned a per week salary that was more than generous. "Now I have to get going, and so do you. Tess, you really have helped me more than you'll ever know. Thank you again."

She saw the sincerity etched on his face and didn't doubt for an instant that his gratitude was heartfelt. She wished she had the same confidence in herself that he seemed to have.

"Luke, if for any reason I can't… I mean, if it doesn't work out…"

Luke held up a hand, stopping her. "It will be okay, Tess. Have faith in yourself and in God. You'll need both to keep up with my son. He's a good kid, but he's all boy."

"Not quite sure about having faith in God, but I'll work on the having faith in me part." She shrugged as she walked Luke to the door and said goodbye. Closing the door softly, she leaned back against it and took a deep breath.

What had she gotten herself into? She had been in town barely two weeks and she already had a puppy and a little boy to take care of. What next? *Not funny, God. I am not amused.*

Twenty minutes later she had the aunts in her car. They arrived at the church just in time for the start of the meeting and were waved to three empty seats in the front of the room by Linda Mason, her chubby face beaming when she spotted them.

"Hi, I saved you some seats. Tess, good to see you."

"We would have been earlier but Tess was talking to Luke and she was our ride," Katie said without rancor.

"We're not late, sister," Annie pointed out, as they took their seats and proceeded to get out notebooks and pens.

"Of course not. I was only saying that we would have been here a while ago. No offense, Tess, dear."

"None taken, Auntie." Tess suppressed a smile as she turned to Linda. "Good to see you, too. I hear the boys, all four of them, are camping in your backyard tonight."

Linda laughed. "Yeah, well, we'll see how that works out for them."

The meeting was called to order, and Tess learned that there was another festival in the works.

Luke was right, this town seemed to have a lot of festivals. In spite of herself, Tess got caught up in the planning of the summer event to benefit the county homeless shelter and food pantry. The aunts were very involved in the planning, throwing out ideas one after the other, not being dissuaded if one of them got shot down. It was fascinating and Tess began to relax, sitting back in her seat and enjoying the show; that was, until she heard Aunt Annie speak.

"May I address the council, Reverend?" Annie inquired politely after raising her hand.

"Of course, Miss Annie, go right ahead." The pastor smiled encouragingly, and she smiled benignly back at him as she stood, clearing her throat.

"Reverend Fulcher and esteemed fellow church members."

Tess looked over at Katie when she heard her groan and mutter, "Oh, no."

"I would like to address the issue of the cakewalk. I want to nominate our niece by marriage, Tess Greenwood, to be in charge of it."

What in the world? Tess sat up in her chair, reaching out a hand to tug on Annie's sleeve. "No," she whispered. "No, Aunt Annie."

Cakewalk? In charge? Not on your life!

Annie smiled down at her, totally ignoring her protests. Tess heard several people in the room clap appreciatively, and slowly took her hand off Annie's clothing.

"I second the nomination!" Linda Mason said, standing.

"I third the nomination, if there is such a thing. Excellent idea, sister." Katie smiled in approval as she stood also.

"I object." Every head in the room turned toward Sarah Fulcher, who had gotten to her feet, as well.

"She's not a member of this church and is hardly qualified to run one of our charity functions." Sarah turned a false little smile in her direction. "No offense, Tess, but it's true."

"Nonsense. She's a member of this church as long as she is here. She's attended services and I'm sure she is happy to help, aren't you, dear?" Katie smiled down at her encouragingly.

Tess was in a state of semishock. What was with this town? Why couldn't they all just leave her alone? Was it really too much to ask? Such a simple thing, really.

"I…" *I what? I can't? I don't want to? I really just want you all to leave me alone?* It all sounded so petty, even to her ears, and if anyone was sympathetic to her own plight, it was her. *Oh, great. Now you sound like an imbecile, to yourself of all people. Happy, God? You know I can't tell them no.*

"Sarah, she is a highly qualified physician assistant with over ten years of experience." Annie was smiling gently at the younger woman as though explaining something to a child.

"What has that got to do with running a cakewalk, Miss Annie?" Sarah asked, a little sharply, Tess thought.

"It speaks of her organizational skills, of course. All in favor of Tess organizing the cakewalk, say aye!"

A resounding "aye" carried through the room, followed by applause.

"Well, isn't that just fine. Tess, you're in charge of the cakewalk!" Aunt Annie was obviously very pleased with the outcome as she patted Tess on the back.

Katie winked at Tess as the group moved on to the

next order of business. Sarah looked more than a little stunned as she retook her seat. *And that's that,* Tess thought. *I have a puppy, a nanny job and am in charge of a church cakewalk, all in the space of two weeks.* She was pretty certain that if she had actively *tried* to get involved with the goings-on in this village, she couldn't have done this well in so short a space of time. *I give up,* she thought faintly as she slumped back in her seat. *I just plain give up.*

"Tess, dear? Are you zoning?"

Tess started. She had been so caught up in her thoughts that she hadn't heard Aunt Katie call her name.

"Um…yes, I'm sorry. What did you say?"

"I said it's time to go home, if you don't mind. The meeting's over, dear."

"Good use of the word *zoning*, sister." Annie smiled approvingly at her twin.

"Thank you, sister. Let's get going, Tess," Katie said, and began to usher the ladies, including a still somewhat shell-shocked Tess, to the door of the community center.

"Come on, Caleb. Get a move on or I'm going to be late for work." Luke picked up the manila envelope with all the information for Tess as he walked to the foot of the stairs.

"I'm coming, Dad! Just gotta get my football in case Miss Tess wants to toss it around with me." Caleb flew down the stairs, football in hand. "Do you think she will? Joey says so. He thinks she's a pretty cool girl and she throws really good. She knocked Mr. Joe in the water."

"I don't know if she's any good at football, son, but be easy on her to start with. We need to keep her around for a while. Got it?"

"Got it. Joey says I lucked out getting Miss Tess to watch me. Do you think we lucked out, too, Dad?"

"I'm pretty sure we lucked out." Luke grinned as he started the truck and backed out of the driveway.

Only God knew if this would work out, but Luke prayed it would with all his heart. Tess had seemed so unsure of herself that a part of him was questioning his decision to leave Caleb with her. He quickly pushed that thought out of his head. He had faith in God, and oddly enough he had faith in Tess. He didn't know her all that well, but what he did know of her he liked. Time would tell if she could cope and if Caleb would be happy with Luke's choice in nanny. His gut told him it would be fine, and he always went with his gut. It had never failed him yet.

Fifteen minutes later he was sitting at Tess's kitchen table, enjoying a cup of coffee and going over the packet he had brought. She needed to be aware of the fact that Caleb was allergic to peanuts. The papers also included his doctor's information in case anything requiring medical aid should happen. Luke had even signed and gotten notarized a document that gave her permission to get Caleb treated, just in case.

"Oh, and another thing. Caleb is not to go near any boat without an adult with him."

"Understood. Does he like boats?" Tess asked.

She was leaning across the table, looking at the papers with him, and he could smell the fresh, clean scent of whatever fragrance she was wearing. He had to admit it was a little distracting, and he fought to concentrate on the task at hand. But, oh, she smelled more than good.

"He does," Luke confirmed, and then went on to explain how Caleb and Joey had been taking the Masons' small Carolina skiff over to visit Shackleford Island.

"Not good," Tess agreed. "I'll be sure to keep a sharp eye out on that front. Is there anything else I need to know about Caleb?"

"No, I think that's it for now. How are you doing?"

"Okay. Still working through the nightmares, but my leg feels much better. Oh, that reminds me. I like to go for a swim in the mornings. It's good therapy for my leg. Can Caleb swim?"

"Like a fish."

"Is it all right if he joins me? I'm Red Cross lifesaver certified and I'll keep him close."

Luke looked out the French doors and watched his son running through the yard with Jack. The kid had so much energy. Any way that he could work it off would be good for him. Tess must have sensed his hesitation.

"I can get my swim in before you get here in the mornings. That's not a problem. I just thought Caleb might like to join me." She shrugged her shoulders slightly, an understanding look on her beautiful face.

"No, no. It's a good idea. I'll put his swim trunks in his bag for tomorrow. I'm sorry if it seems like I'm being overly cautious. I'm new at this father gig and have had to learn so many things by trial and error over the past six months." Luke stood. "And now I have to get to work. Again, Tess, thank you. I should be by to pick him up around four-thirty or so."

"That's fine, take your time. And by the way, you're not being overly cautious, Luke. You're being a good parent," she called over her shoulder as she went to the kitchen door. "Caleb, bring Jack in and come say goodbye to your dad. He has to leave now."

The boy flew through the door, Jack in his arms.

"She went potty, Miss Tess. I made sure. I told her that she wasn't allowed to use the floor anymore. I'm pretty sure she won't now."

"I appreciate that, Caleb. I hope she listens to you." Tess smiled.

"Hey, Dad, you leaving?" Caleb asked.

"Yep, buddy. Have to get going. Be good and mind Miss Tess. Take care of each other. Got it?"

"Got it, Gunny! I'll take good care of Miss Tess and Jack. Promise. Just like I took good care of Mom." The little boy snapped a smart salute, which Luke returned.

He was surprised at the mention of Jennifer. Today had been one of the few times he had heard Caleb comment on his mother. Luke swallowed past the lump that had formed in his throat at the thought of his son dealing with a terminally ill mother at such a young age. The boy had been through so much.

"Good deal. I'm counting on you. Both of you," he added, looking at Tess as he spoke.

"Got it, Gunny," she said softly.

He gave a short nod. *Lord, take care of both of them,* he prayed as he walked out the door.

Chapter Nine

"So here's what I've found out since our last meeting. Grandparents do have certain rights in the state of Tennessee. They can petition the court for custody in certain instances."

Luke nodded shortly as he took in what the lawyer was saying. The news wasn't what he had hoped to hear. When he'd made the appointment with base legal to discuss the custody situation, he had hoped that they would tell him Jen's parents didn't have a leg to stand on.

"And what are those instances?"

"Bear in mind, Gunny, that if the court grants a hearing, they are trying to determine what is in the best interests of the child."

"I want what's in his best interests, as well, Major. This isn't about me, it's all about him, but I don't want to lose him. So what are the criteria for them to petition?"

"If one of the parents is deceased, which applies here, and they can prove that you are not a fit parent. That's not an easy thing to do. There is something called the parental preference rule. Fit parents who are able and willing to care for their child have the principal right to the custody, care and nurturing of the child rather than any third person. The rule is a huge barrier for the grandparents and works to your advantage."

Luke felt a small bit of hope. Proving he wasn't a fit parent would be difficult for them, but they would be digging for anything they could use against him, he knew. He had worked hard to make a good home for Caleb, but what if his son wanted to live with his grandparents? Luke hadn't brought the subject up for fear Caleb would say he did. He was close to them and the move here hadn't been easy. To go somewhere he had never been and live with a father he had never known had to be hard. Add to that the fact that he had just lost his mother... The kid's whole world had turned upside down.

"I've never asked Caleb what he wanted," Luke admitted to the lawyer. "Should I? Or is he too young to make that decision on his own?" For the first time since Dave had told him that they wanted custody, Luke felt a twinge of uncertainty.

"The court will certainly want to talk to Caleb and take his wishes into consideration. Have you told him that his grandparents are petitioning for custody? And have you heard from their lawyer yet?"

"No and no."

"Perhaps it would be a good idea to speak with Caleb before the petition becomes a reality. Ask him how he feels about living with you. Be honest and tell him what his grandparents want. That way, when or if it comes down, at least he won't be taken by surprise."

Luke didn't answer immediately. It wasn't fair to keep Caleb from knowing what was going on, because it concerned him. But Luke had thought him too young and wanted to shield him. Maybe ten wasn't too young. Maybe he was making a mistake by not saying anything.

"I think you might be right, sir. I'll have a talk with him this evening." Luke rubbed the back of his neck tiredly. "Parenting isn't an easy job."

"No, but it's the most rewarding job in the world. I've got three of my own. You'll get there, Gunny. From where I'm sitting and from everything you've told me, you're doing a good job for someone who just became the father of a ten-year-old boy. Someone with no experience, I might add." The major leaned back in his chair as he spoke and smiled encouragingly.

"I'm trying. He seems to be settling in well now. He has friends and is involved in sports and Scouting."

"How's your relationship with him?"

"It was rough at first, still is some days." Luke admitted. "But now, within the past month or so, we seem to be getting closer. He's laughing a lot more and talking a mile a minute, but we still have days that are tough for both of us."

"It all takes time. So, as your lawyer, I think your best course of action is to talk to him and wait. We'll be ready if they actually do petition the courts. Right now it's just rhetoric. The fact that his mother wanted him to be with you speaks volumes."

"Thank you, sir." Luke stood and shook the major's hand before leaving the office.

Once out in the bright sunshine, he took a deep breath. The lawyer was right; for whatever reason, Jennifer had wanted him to take care of Caleb. Luke wished she had left him a letter or something, anything to give him insight into her decision—*both* of her decisions. The choice not to tell him she was pregnant, and then later, when she knew she was dying, the choice to give him custody. The will hadn't given any indication as to why. It was time to call Caleb's grandparents and have a talk about all this, and then talk to Caleb.

Luke didn't know which conversation he was dreading more. Dave had been furious when he had found out that Luke had taken the phone from Caleb, so he didn't expect the discussion would go well. But the conversation with Caleb… What if Luke talked to him and found out that Caleb didn't want to live with him, after all?

"So, my dear, as promised, here's the list of ladies who have volunteered to make the cakes for the summer fair. The phone numbers are next to the names. And the rest is a piece of cake!" Annie chuckled at her own joke, while Katie rolled her eyes.

Tess reached for the paper. The list looked awfully long.

"It took some persuading to pry the list out of Sarah's hot little hands, but we managed, as we always do when confronted with an immovable object. She was in charge last year. I think everyone was ready for a bit of a change."

Katie smiled gently as she reached for the lemonade that sat in front of her.

"She really put up quite an argument. I have to hand it to her." Annie shook her head, a look of admiration on her face. "She doesn't seem to like you much, dear, which I told her was ridiculous, as she doesn't know you at all."

"I got the same feeling," Tess murmured. She was at a loss as to what the other woman's problem with her was. "I hate to ask, but what exactly is a cakewalk? I mean, it would help if I knew what I was doing."

"It's very simple," Katie said with a kind look. "The ladies on the list will bake the treats needed. You'll need music, chairs and, of course, participants. It's like musical chairs with the winners getting a baked good of one kind or another."

"It's not restricted to just cakes. You can have all sorts of homemade treats! We'll help you, not to worry." Annie smiled.

"As for Sarah, her problem has everything to do with Luke and the fact that you are quite lovely. Competition." Katie took a long sip of lemonade. "By the way, dear, very good lemonade. Use a bit less sugar next time, though. Not quite tart enough."

"Competition? I'm no rival when it comes to Luke's affections. That doesn't make sense."

After all, what man in his right mind would be interested in a woman with so much baggage, emotionally and physically? the little voice in her head said. *But it would be nice to have someone care for you in that way.* She pushed the thought away almost before it formed.

It wasn't going to happen with Luke or any other man, at least not anytime soon.

"You should have seen her face when she found out that you're caring for Caleb! Priceless, simply priceless." Annie chortled at the memory. "Don't get me wrong, Tess, we love her very much. Known her all of her life. She's a good soul, but just a wee bit spoiled."

"A *wee* bit?" Katie arched a brow at her sister. "A *lot* bit! Her parents indulge her far too much. And seriously, at twenty-eight she should have started making her way in the world, on her own. I can't fathom why they haven't pushed her out of the nest by now."

"Only child. Only children are extremely close to Momma and Daddy," Annie stated, nodding wisely.

"Well, if the cakewalk means so much to her, she can have it back. I really don't have a problem with that at all." Tess's words were heartfelt and she gave the aunts a sincere look.

She still felt she had been railroaded into the position, though she didn't want to let them down by backing out. But if Sarah was so bent around the axle about it, she could definitely take over again. Maybe this was Tess's out. She looked over at Caleb, sitting in the hot-pink golf cart, with Jack on the seat beside him.

"Oh, no. It's all been finalized," Katie declared. "You have the cakewalk. Sarah will survive. I'm so glad that you decided to take Caleb for Luke, by the way. Everything going okay?" Then she called over to Caleb, "Dear, please don't turn the key. Don't want any accidents, there's a good boy."

Rats! Well, you tried. Halfheartedly, but you did try.

Tess tried to look as if nothing was amiss, but wasn't sure that she had succeeded. It didn't matter, anyway, because the sisters were gazing at Caleb and not her. The boy gave Katie a thumbs-up as he turned the steering wheel, driving in his imagination to parts known only to him. Jack seemed happy to be along for the ride.

"Hang on, Jack. That was a big hole!" he said to the dog. Jack looked up at him, panting happily.

It was good for the puppy to have a playmate, someone who was able to run around with her. Now if she could just get the training issues straight. Jack still hadn't a clue as to what the puppy pads on the kitchen floor were for, choosing instead to sleep on them.

"He's the most adorable boy, just like his daddy!" Annie smiled dreamily when she mentioned Luke. "Don't you think Luke is adorable, Tess?"

Tess didn't know what to say. *Adorable* wouldn't be a word she would have chosen to describe him. He was certainly handsome in a rugged sort of way. Definitely charming, especially when he leveled that crooked grin in her direction. But Tess had always been a woman who looked past the physical. When she looked at Luke she saw kindness, compassion, empathy and consideration. He had certainly shown her those traits in spades since she had known him. No, *adorable* wasn't the word. And she still couldn't figure out why he seemed so comfortingly familiar, or why she couldn't place him. She had been racking her brain trying to figure it out, but all she got for her efforts was a headache.

"He is handsome, Aunt Annie, and he seems to be a good man. As far as Caleb, everything appears to be going well, but this is the first day. I worry that there isn't enough to do here and he'll get bored before much longer. Up to now, he and Joey have had each other to play with." It *had* been a valid concern of hers, but Luke had brushed it aside, which was just what the aunts were doing now.

"Nonsense, dear. There's plenty to do. Why don't you take him down to the dock and go crabbing? There's a net in the shed, along with fishing poles. There's always the boat and swimming, of course. You do know how to operate a boat, don't you?" Katie didn't wait for an answer before continuing, "And if you're really concerned, ask Linda if you can have Joey over, as well, at least for a couple of days during the week."

Katie took another sip of the insufficiently tart lemonade, looking at Tess over the rim of the glass as if to say, *So what's the problem? It's nothing to take care of two boys*.

Two boys? Good grief. Tess barely knew what to do with one. No, no, no. It wasn't possible. Period. She liked Joey and his parents, but taking on another child could put her in over her head. Way over her head.

"No, I don't think that's a very good idea," she began, but as usual, neither of the aunts was listening to her.

"As always, brilliant idea, sister. I'll call Linda's cell now." Annie was grinning from ear to ear as she pulled up the number from her phone's address book.

"Of course it's brilliant, sister. Most of my ideas are, as you well know. Oh, that reminds me. Tess, did we mention that the garden club would like to have its monthly luncheon in the garden here? It's so lovely.

We've had it on the calendar for months. I meant to tell you. The moon gate adds so much to the ambience. We have it here at least once a year."

"No, you didn't mention it," Tess said faintly as she took the phone that Annie was pressing into her hand.

"Tess?" Linda Mason's voice sounded in her ear.

"Er… Hi, Linda."

Tess really was at a loss. How had so much happened in so short a period? It seemed that every time the aunts were involved, she could add something else to what was becoming a long list of must dos. She just didn't know how to tell them no. They had been so kind to her since her arrival that it seemed petty of her not to lend a hand. And they were only trying to be helpful, arranging a playdate with Joey and Caleb.

But you have to draw the line somewhere, she told herself.

Then Livie's words came back to her: *"They find causes and champion them. They take in strays. Everything they do for you is predicated with love."*

Did they see her as a cause to champion? It certainly looked that way.

"Annie says you want to take Joey, as well? Isn't that a bit much for you?"

Yes, but how do I say no? Tess couldn't say the words out loud, knowing she would be shot down by the Salters, who were listening avidly to the conversation.

"Well, it would be if it were every day. Maybe once or twice a week, just to give Caleb someone other than the dog to play with around here." Tess sighed, not realizing she was doing so until both aunts looked at her sharply.

"Not your idea? No problem. I know what the sisters are like when it comes to ideas and plans." Linda chucked softly.

"Thank you, Linda. Thank you!" Tess couldn't keep the relief out of her voice. "But I do think it's a good idea for Joey to come over at some point during the week," she added.

"Why don't we try Wednesdays to begin with. Chances are the boys will see each other over the weekend, anyway. This gives them a couple of days apart before they get together again."

"Sounds good." Tess looked at the aunts, who were nodding in agreement to the portion of the dialogue they were privy to.

"See how easy that was? There is a solution to every problem." Annie took the phone back from Tess and squeezed her hand encouragingly. "At least we like to think so."

"And now we need to discuss the garden club luncheon. Not to worry, dear, you'll not have to lift a finger. It will be catered and all of the tables and chairs will be set up a day ahead. Of course, Annie and I will be here on Friday to make sure everything goes smoothly, and we do expect you to attend. I think we have around forty people confirmed." Aunt Katie had put a pair of spectacles on before she took a notebook out of her handbag.

"Friday. This Friday?" Tess almost squeaked the question.

"Yes, this Friday. The luncheon is on Saturday, setup is Friday. Is there a problem?" Annie smiled benignly at her.

"No, no problem. I just thought there would be more time to prepare."

Tess leaned back in her chair. *It is what it is*, she thought. Part of her was amazed at the vitality that these two seventy-something women possessed. The other part of her felt as if a tsunami had hit the cottage the moment they had arrived. You couldn't stop it; it was an inevitable force of nature. She was no match for them, and however she felt didn't seem to matter. She was learning that wherever the aunts went, they were an energy to be reckoned with. Her only course of action at this point was to sit back and let them do as they pleased.

"You don't have to prepare anything. Just enjoy the luncheon with us. It really is a lovely affair with good company. It will be good for you. You don't get out much and this will give you a chance to meet some new people that don't attend our church. Speaking of which, I do wish you would start attending services on a more regular basis. Especially since you're in charge of the cakewalk. So I expect we'll see you there this Sunday." Katie looked at her over the rims of her glasses and then glanced down at her notebook as she wrote something on the paper, not waiting for an answer, as usual. It was a statement, not a question.

But Tess did answer and was surprised to hear herself say, "Yes, Auntie. I'll be there."

Might as well. She mentally shrugged. It wasn't as if

her Sundays were booked solid for the rest of her stay in the village. She still couldn't find it in her to reconcile herself to God's will, but attending services didn't necessarily mean that she agreed with Him. It was for the aunts, she assured herself. Nothing more, nothing less.

"Now we have to get going. I'm sure Luke will be here soon to collect Caleb."

"No, sister, he won't be here until after four-thirty." Annie stood up as she spoke, then kissed Tess on the cheek. Katie followed suit, leaning down with a genuine smile as she gazed into Tess's eyes.

"Life is good, dear. Don't you ever forget that," she whispered into her ear, before kissing her softly on the other cheek. "And how do you know what time Luke will be home?" She looked at her sister as she straightened up.

Tess bit her lip, her eyes tearing up a little at Aunt Katie's words. Life had always been good before. She just hoped she could find the good parts again. She knew they were there, somewhere. Her eyes strayed over to Caleb as he got out of the golf cart. It *was* good to have both him and Jack with her. She had had far less time to think about the accident and to question God's part in it while they were around. Far less time to grieve over the loss of so many innocent lives. Her heart did feel lighter today. She hoped with everything inside her that the healing had truly begun.

"Luke told me after church yesterday. I was curious as to how long Caleb would be with Tess during the day. No biggie." Annie ruffled the boy's hair as she got into the cart next to her sister.

"No biggie?" Katie started the cheery vehicle and looked at her twin askance.

"Right, no big deal. That's what that means, sister."

"I'll try to remember that one. Annie May, you do come up with phrases I have never heard before. You always have."

"Keeps us young, don't you think?" Annie smiled and waved as the golf cart bounced down the lane.

"I'm starved, Miss Tess! What's for dinner?" Caleb ran over to her, his blue eyes shining. He seemed to be having a good day, as well, and Tess smiled at him.

"Roast chicken and veggies. Come help me put the chicken on. Come, Jack."

Tess watched as the puppy squatted and piddled on the grass next to the terrace. Well, that was good. At least it wasn't in the hallway. Jack was having a good day, too, it seemed.

Chapter Ten

Luke pulled the truck into a gas station parking lot, put it in Park and took out his cell phone. He wanted to have the conversation with Caleb's grandfather without Caleb around to overhear. Luke was normally a very calm and controlled man, but he wasn't sure how the conversation would go, and if he raised his voice it might frighten his son. That was the last thing he wanted.

He was planning to tell Caleb what was going on, but first needed to find out exactly what Dave and Katherine were planning on doing. Luke hadn't heard anything from them since the threat to petition for custody, and frankly, he was getting tired of waiting for the other shoe to drop. He dialed the number and put the phone to his ear. Dave answered on the first ring.

"Knew you'd be calling. First of all, why did you take my grandson's cell phone away from him?" No "Hello, how are you?" Just jump right in. Luke took a breath. This combative tone was not the way he wanted to begin.

"Dave, he's too young to have a cell phone."

"Humph. Well, now he doesn't have an escape route."

"Escape route? What are you talking about? Caleb doesn't need a way to escape." Luke fought to keep his voice reasonable.

"Right. He's ten years old and miles from everything and everyone he knows. Tell me he's happy." Dave scoffed at the very idea.

"I'd say he is, or at least he's getting there. Has he told you otherwise? He can and has called you anytime he feels like it. Has he told you he is unhappy?"

"Well, no," the older man conceded, "but that's not the point. The point is that he should be living here with his grandma and me. Not with you, who never came around him once in his life."

"Hard to come around when I never knew he existed. You know as well as I do that Jen never told me about him. If she had, everything would be different."

"Yeah, we told her not to tell you. The only time in her life she ever listened to us. She sure didn't listen when I told her not to marry you. She learned her lesson the hard way there. Came running home to her mother and me, just like I told her she would. Should have been grateful we took her back, but no. She up and took the boy away from us. We tried to get him back, prove that she was an unfit mother, couldn't care for him like we could. But the court said no. Well, this time, we will get him. We can prove you're not a fit father. Leaving him with a physically and mentally incompetent woman while you're at work. You made a huge mistake there!" Dave practically spat the words out, his tone hard and gritty.

The man sounded positively hateful and Luke had to stop himself from reacting with anger. Anger got you nowhere. He had learned that years ago. Then the harsh words sank in. They had tried to take Caleb from Jen? But why? Luke knew with everything in him that Jen had been a good mother. She had always been a kind, nurturing woman. And even though the boy didn't often speak of her, Luke could tell that Caleb had adored her.

Then another thought struck him. Physically and mentally incompetent woman? Tess? How did Dave know about Tess, and where did he get the idea she was incompetent? Couldn't have been from Caleb. As far as Luke knew, he hadn't spoken to his grandparents in the past few days. And Caleb had only ever had good things to say about Tess.

"Dave, how do you know who's caring for my son?" Luke kept his tone even as he asked the question.

"If you must know, your girlfriend, the preacher's daughter, told me all about it."

"Sarah? Sarah Fulcher? How do you know her?" *And why do you think she's my girlfriend?* To say Luke was surprised was an understatement.

"I did some checking when you told me you and the boy were going to church. I called the church you mentioned to see if it was true. Your girlfriend answered the phone. Been talking to her for a few months now. Mighty nice young lady. Keeps us informed on what's going on with you and my grandson."

White-hot anger shot through Luke like a bolt of

lightning. He couldn't recall ever being so furious. What was Sarah playing at? Why hadn't she told him that Caleb's grandparents had called the church? And how dare she discuss Luke's private affairs behind his back? He fought hard to get himself under control. He didn't speak for a minute or two as he tried to gather his thoughts. Again, anger was not the answer. Anger only made things worse and was a wasted emotion. It drained a body, sucked the life right out of you. Anger had no place in dealing with his son's future.

Lord, help me. Please help me get through this without anger, without malice toward anyone. Please help me to understand what Sarah was trying to accomplish in not telling me.

"Dave, first of all, Tess Greenwood, my son's child care provider, is not incompetent in any way. Just the opposite. She's a physician assistant, and is highly qualified to care for Caleb. Secondly, Sarah Fulcher is not my girlfriend. I have no idea what she's been telling you, and quite frankly at this point I don't care. Caleb is well taken care of. He couldn't be more loved and has made new friends since his move here. Sure, he's had to make adjustments and things haven't always been smooth, but we're getting there. It's new for both of us, but we are going to make it."

Luke stopped at that point, waiting for the older man to speak. He felt a sense of peace after his short prayer asking God to help him control the anger he felt. It had been a gut reaction. He knew he had done nothing wrong when it came to Caleb, and he refused to be blackmailed into giving him up.

"We'll just see about that. I'm doing a background check on that woman and I warn you, if anything— and I mean anything—not on the up-and-up comes back on her, I *will* file to take custody away from you. You haven't heard the last of this issue," the older man warned.

"I'm sure I haven't, but you know what? Why don't you and Katherine come here and visit with Caleb, if only to satisfy yourselves that he is doing well? I have plenty of room at the house and he would be happy to see you. We have nothing to hide. Just as I'm sure that Jen wanted you to be in Caleb's life, I want the same."

Luke spoke quietly and calmly, his voice laced with sincerity. But once again, a small nagging doubt crept into his mind about Tess. Was there anything in her background that he should have known about before leaving Caleb in her care? Normally, he would have run a background check himself on any person he left his son with. With Tess, he had assumed, since he knew her family, that all was well. Besides, there hadn't been time. He had needed help quickly and she had stepped up to the plate when he had asked her to. No, he couldn't believe he would find anything to darken his opinion of her, no matter how hard he looked. Tess was a beautiful soul and he was blessed to have found her again, blessed in more ways than one.

Silence greeted his words for a moment before the older man spoke. "If my daughter had wanted us in the boy's life, she would never have moved out of this house. And then she went and got cancer and really couldn't take care of him properly. We tried to get him back, but the courts told us no—just because she was sick didn't make her an unfit mother. Then she up and died…" His voice trailed off.

Luke heard the pain in the man's voice and felt a sharp stab of compassion for him. The loss of Jennifer had been hard for Caleb and hard for her parents, as well. When he had learned about her passing, he, too, had grieved for the vivacious woman he had loved in his youth. She had been so full of life, so warm and giving. And she had bequeathed him Caleb, the greatest gift he had ever received. He would be forever grateful to her for that, even though he knew her choice had hurt her parents deeply.

There had to be some sort of resolution that would satisfy Caleb's grandparents, and he was working hard to find it without going through a court battle. He refused to give up his son, unless that was what Caleb wanted. Luke's greatest fear was that the boy would say yes, he wanted to go back to Tennessee.

Luke knew what he had to do. He dreaded the conversation with Caleb, but it had to happen. He took a deep breath before he spoke, choosing his words carefully as he stared unseeing at the traffic moving along the highway in front of him.

"I think it's only fair that I ask Caleb what he wants. If he's not happy here with me, and wishes to go back and live with you, I won't stop him. His happiness is what matters. It's what he wants that counts, not what you or I want." Luke's shoulders slumped a little as he spoke. He was suddenly very tired.

"How do I know you won't try to influence him?" the man asked skeptically.

"You have my word," Luke answered simply. "Take it for what it's worth, and in my book, it's worth quite a bit. Is it a deal?"

"Don't see why you have to drag the boy into this. He's not old enough to know what he wants."

"I disagree. And since the decision involves him, he has every right to know what's going on. Is it a deal?" Luke didn't mean to sound sharp, but talking to the older man was like talking to a tree. He was immovable, set on what he believed to be right and seemingly not willing to compromise.

"I'm not saying it's a deal until after I get the background check on that Greenwood woman. If everything is good, talk to the boy and ask him what he wants. If it's not, I'll go to court and get custody. That's my deal."

"All right, Dave. I'll wait until you get the report on Tess. After that, I handle it my way and talk to Caleb."

"Up to you. I'll be in touch." With that, the man hung up.

Luke slammed the steering wheel with his fist. He hated the anger that had welled up in him once again as Caleb's grandfather hung up on him. Why was Dave being so stubborn? It was nothing new, though. He had been this way when Luke and Jen had gotten married, refusing to come to the wedding. Katherine had been there to support Jen, but Dave had stayed away, claiming it would not last. The worst of it was that he had been right.

Luke looked at his watch and sighed before he started

the truck. It was past time to pick up Caleb. He hoped
that Caleb and Tess's day had been better than his.

"My mom always let me help her, too. I like to cook."
Caleb took the mixing bowl from Tess and put it in the
sink as he spoke. "No, Jack. It's not for puppies. It's
people food."

Tess's felt her heart contract at the boy's words. He
must miss his mother so much. They were in the kitchen
putting the finishing touches on a lemon pie that she
had prepared for dessert. Caleb had been watching her
closely as she moved around the kitchen, so she had told
him that she needed help. He had jumped right in, bit-
ing his lower lip in concentration as she'd handed him
the mixer to whip the pie filling.

"Well, you did a super job on the pie! I don't know
how I would have gotten everything done without your
help." Tess smiled gently as she spoke. "So your mom
taught you how to cook?"

"Yep. When she got sick, I used to make her soup
and a sandwich. She loved pimento cheese. Do you like
pimento cheese sandwiches? I can always make you
one, if you like 'em, that is."

He really was a well-behaved child, and having him
here with her had been good for her, Tess realized. Her
day had been filled with purpose, something she had
not known for a long time. Too long of a time. Her heart
felt lighter than it had in months.

"I'd love for someone to make me a pimento cheese
sandwich. I don't think anyone has ever made me one."

"Mom said mine were the best."

"Then I'm sure I'll love them." Tess hesitated before her next words. "You must really miss your mom a lot, Caleb."

"I do." He nodded emphatically. "She got cancer and she had to leave me, but she said that when she died, to always remember she would be with me, in here." He touched his chest as he looked seriously at Tess. "I used to be mad at God, like Grampy is, but now I'm not. My dad taught me that God is all-loving, so it makes sense that Mom would be with Him. She's all-loving, too."

Tess paused, his words sinking into the depths of her soul. They were almost her undoing. How a ten-year-old child could cope with the death of his beloved mother so sweetly and simply, with such blind faith, was beyond her. She had allowed herself to become mired in the deaths of the children at the orphanage, not allowing herself to try to understand. Instead of falling back on her faith, she had fought against it.

She wished that she could accept God's will with the blind faith of a child, but she just couldn't. Not yet, not now. She realized then that He had put this incredibly beautiful young soul in her life to show her the way home. She wasn't quite ready to follow that road, but she knew she was a step closer. Looking at the earnest little face in front of her, she almost believed he was right. She almost believed that God was all-loving and that she shouldn't question His will. Caleb had certainly given her food for thought, and she felt so much compassion for the young boy at that moment that she almost cried. Instead, she held out her arms, and Caleb ran into them without hesitation.

She hugged him tightly. "Yes, dear Caleb, she will always be with you."

Breaking the hug, she got down on her knees in front of him and touched his chest. "Right here."

"Can I go look through the telescope now?" Caleb asked, an eager look on his face.

"Yes, you may. Your dad should be here soon. I need to get dinner finished up." Tess got to her feet as she spoke, after giving Caleb one last hug. "Thank you, Caleb."

"What did I do?" he asked, giving her a puzzled look.

"You helped me to put something that has been bothering me into perspective."

"What's perspective?"

"Something I've been lacking for a long time. I'll explain it all to you one day, promise. For now, let's just say that you are exactly what I needed right now."

"Oh, well, you're welcome, then. Glad I could help, ma'am."

He looked and sounded so much like Luke when he said it that Tess had to smile as she watched him pick up Jack and head for the upstairs porch and the telescope. Suddenly, he paused and turned around.

"I think you're exactly what my dad and me needed, too, Miss Tess." With that he was gone, before she could ask him what he meant.

Twenty minutes later, Tess went to find Caleb. His dad would be home soon and she wasn't sure whether they would be eating here or if she needed to pack up the meal to go. Either way, it had been good to cook for someone other than herself.

Her mind wandered. *Home.* She had a fleeting vision of Luke coming home after work, to her and a house filled with children, Caleb's brothers and sisters. *Whoa. Where did that come from?* She shook her head. Silly to even have the thought. *But what if...just what if?* a little voice asked her as she tried to push the thought away as quickly as it came. If she had been in any other place in her life, she would have let herself wonder, but not now.

Still, you are attracted to him, and so is every woman in this lovely, quirky village. Hard not to be. Ruggedly handsome, big and strong. Looks great in a uniform. But those were not good reasons for her attraction to him, though his looks didn't hurt. He was intelligent, kind and compassionate and had a strong faith in God, and although she was struggling with her own faith, those were the reasons she was drawn to him. She sighed as she went onto the porch overlooking the front yard and saw Caleb peering through the telescope intently.

"What are you looking at?"

"Me and Joey's island. You can see it real good from up here with the telescope. Look." He moved so she could position herself in front of the lens.

"Joey's and my island," she absentmindedly corrected him, as she took a peek through the telescope. "It's beautiful."

"Yep. That's our pirate island. I love it over there. It's way cool! We hunted for treasure and collected booty.

Well, shells mostly, but sometimes we find sea glass on the beach, and sand dollars. We even have a pirate map we drew of the island and we buried our treasure there, but don't tell anyone."

"I promise not to tell a soul. We wouldn't want anyone to find your treasure." Tess held up her hand as a pledge as she thought of all the wonderful adventures little boys have.

"But we can't go there now."

"Isn't that because you were taking the boat without adult supervision?" she asked gently.

Caleb nodded and his cheeks turned red, as though he was embarrassed that she knew. The look on his face tugged at her heart.

"Well, how about if I ask your dad if I can take you over to the island one day?" Tess didn't think it would hurt to ask. She certainly knew how to handle a boat, having grown up on Puget Sound. Her family were avid boaters.

"Really, Miss Tess? For real? Would you take both Joey and me? That would be so cool!"

"I'll talk to him," she said. "No promises on what he'll say, though."

"Talk to me about what?"

Tess must have jumped ten feet. She whirled around and saw Luke standing on the porch behind them. Her heart did a slow flip and ended up somewhere in the region of her tummy as she took in the handsome face etched with what could only be described as a tired smile. Tired though it was, it still had the power to wreak havoc on her psyche, especially considering her earlier thoughts about him.

"Dad!" Caleb gave a loud whoop as Tess leaned against the porch railing for the support she suddenly needed.

Chapter Eleven

"So that's where I stand as far as custody goes."

Luke leaned back in his seat tiredly before taking a drink of the coffee Tess had provided after dinner, to go with the delicious pie. The meal had been wonderful. He remembered with pleasure approaching the welcoming house, filled with scrumptious smells and two of his favorite people in the world. It felt so much like home that he had allowed himself the fleeting daydream of it really being home, his home, with his son and Tess waiting for him at the end of a long workday. But he pushed the fantasy aside as quickly as it had come. He was more than a little attracted to her, but knew in his head that as a couple, they would be impossible for the time being. She was working through so many issues right now and his priority was Caleb. But still, the thought warmed him.

In his heart, he yearned for a wife and children. He hadn't been able to make things work with Jen but he was determined to get it right with Caleb. His son was his priority. There was no room for anyone else but the two of them.

Nevertheless, he found himself confiding to Tess about the issues with custody. He was normally a private man when it came to personal matters, but there was something about Tess that invited confidences. She was warm and understanding, not interrupting as he spoke, and once he started, it all came tumbling out. Even the bits about her supposedly being incompetent, and Sarah's part in speaking to Caleb's grandfather.

He couldn't have stopped if he had wanted to. It was healing to share what was going on. He hadn't realized until then how worried he really was about his son being taken from him. Sharing with the military attorney was different. No emotions involved. Even sharing with Mike was different, he was so far removed from the situation. Sharing with the woman sitting across from him, he allowed his feelings to show.

Her green eyes were shadowed with concern and sympathy, and she didn't seem to be at all offended by the unflattering bits about her. For just a moment, he again let himself wonder what it would be like to love her and have her love him back. He shook his head slightly, clearing the thought.

"Well, first of all, nothing negative will come in from a background check on me, so please don't worry about that. I've been through a ton of them as a PA. Secondly, if you were concerned about me watching your son, I suspect you never would have asked me. You of all people know about what I'm dealing with as far as PTSD goes."

Her words were sensible, and he nodded in agreement. "Thanks for the reassurance on the background check. He said he wasn't going to file unless I had been negligent in Caleb's care. I think that's really his only leg to stand on. The courts won't listen to his case unless he can prove that I'm not a fit parent."

"If he really thinks you aren't, then he doesn't know you at all. Anyone can tell that your son is your heart, no matter that he's only been with you for six months. It's obvious that you love him and he adores you."

"He does?" Luke couldn't keep his surprise from showing.

"He does," Tess said firmly. "He talks about you all of the time. 'My dad taught me this, my dad says that.' Like it or not, Luke, you are your son's hero, and what a wonderful thing to be."

Luke's heart swelled at her words. He really hadn't realized that Caleb felt that way. Oh, he knew the boy was adjusting, but becoming a family had been and still was a learning process for both of them. Having validation that that his son really cared for him and looked up to him meant everything, and made all the adjustments, the give-and-take moments, worthwhile.

"Thanks for sharing that with me. It means a lot."

"He's a good kid, Luke, but then you know that."

"Dad!"

Luke and Tess both looked toward the living room as they heard the frantic note in Caleb's voice. Luke got up and rushed to his son. Something was wrong, very wrong. Caleb had gone back to the upstairs porch to take a last look through the telescope before they left for home. Luke didn't realize that Tess was right behind him until he stopped short at the foot of the stairs and she ran into the back of him.

"Caleb?"

"Dad, hurry. It's Grampy!"

Grampy? But he had just spoken with him on the phone that afternoon. Dave was in Tennessee, wasn't he? What was Caleb talking about? Luke took the stairs two at a time, reaching the porch in seconds. Looking down from the balcony, he saw the older man lying facedown on the velvety green lawn next to the front walkway with Sarah kneeling next to him. He wasn't moving.

Luke turned to his son and saw the worried look on his young face. Then his gaze caught Tess's expression, which was shadowed with concern. Luke knew in an instant what he had to do. Adrenaline kicked in as his mind cleared and a plan of action formed. He had always been clearheaded in emergency situations.

He reached in his pocket and pulled out his cell phone, dialing 911. He gave the dispatcher directions and then clicked off and put it away, knowing it would be some time before they arrived. Luke hustled the other two down the stairs. He paused in the living room and looked deep into Tess's eyes. "You have to come and help," he said simply.

"Luke, I don't think I…"

He caught the anxiety in her whisper and put his hands firmly on her slender shoulders. "You can and you will. Reach deep inside of you, Tess, and push the panic away. Fight it."

Her eyes were clouding over with fear and he knew his words weren't getting through to her. In fact, she seemed to be on the verge of a panic attack. He had to say something to shock her enough to snap out of it. And even though this was the last way he would have wanted to tell her, he knew there was only one thing he could say.

"You're a fighter, Tess. I knew it when I pulled you out of that orphanage and walked down that mountain with you in my arms."

He watched her closely, seeing the realization dawn in her lovely eyes. He would talk to her about it later. Right now they needed her medical expertise for Dave.

"Caleb, there's a small black bag in the closet behind you. Grab it for me, please." That was all she said as she nodded sharply at Luke. If she was angry at him for not telling her sooner, he would deal with it afterward.

"Got it, Miss Tess. I think it's his ticker. Grampy has a bad one. Do you think it's his ticker, Miss Tess?"

"I won't know until I get out there. Let's go."

"Are you a doctor?" the boy asked as they hurried through the front door.

"No, but I might be able to help."

At least it's still light out, she thought. It was early evening and the sun had yet to set. *God, please help me to help this man. I'm scared. I haven't done this in a long time. Please be with us and with Caleb's grandfather.* The heartfelt prayer came easily to her and she immediately felt a sense of calm come over her, as she always had in the past when she asked for God's intervention. Part of her was surprised by her prayer, but another part wasn't really surprised at all. Caleb had planted the seed in her heart earlier in the day. The medical emergency was the catalyst that brought her full circle. It had been a long time since she had felt that kind of peace in connection with her life.

Her mind turned to Luke for a second. The marine. He was the marine who had saved her life. Why hadn't he said anything? No wonder he seemed so familiar, especially his voice. How could she have not made the connection?

Easy. You were so immersed in yourself, you totally missed it.

She honestly didn't know what to think or feel. Part of her was angry that he hadn't said anything. It might have helped her to know that he *had* been there that day and knew exactly what had happened. It might have helped her get through a few things that she had been struggling with for the past eight months. In fact, the more she thought of it, the more confused and angry she got.

Let it go. He must have had his reasons, rational Tess told her.

But he lied by omission, irrational Tess countered.

He didn't lie, he just didn't say anything. Rational Tess again.

Same difference, irrational Tess tossed back.

She didn't have time to take the matter further as she reached the elderly man lying on the ground. She felt the old panicky feeling return as she knelt next to him. Taking a deep breath, she ordered herself to carry on. The man needed help and she was the only game in town right now. She noted distantly that Sarah Fulcher looked frightened as she backed away to make room for Tess.

"He got out of the car and just keeled over. Is he dead?"

Tess threw her a sharp glance, willing her to shut up. Caleb was standing silently next to her, a worried expression on his face.

"Luke, help me turn him over." Tess looked up at him as she spoke in a distant, professional tone.

He knelt next to her and they rolled Caleb's grandfather over as carefully as they could. He was a large man and deadweight right now. She searched for a pulse and breathed a sigh of relief when she found it. It was weak, but he was still alive, and complaining! Complaining?

"Get your hands offa me." The words were gravelly and low, but he was talking! Tess felt a wave of relief. If he was talking, he had air.

"Sir, I'm here to help you."

"Don't need no help, girl." The grizzled old man wheezed as he squinted up at her from below white, bushy eyebrows.

"I'd say you do." Tess kept her voice calm as she took in his pallor. She did a quick visual assessment and noticed he was sweating, as well.

"Grampy, you gotta let her help you. She's a medical something, but not a doctor. You don't like doctors. She isn't one, I promise." Caleb knelt down next to the old man and took his hand. Tess saw the man's gaze swing to the boy.

"Where'd you come from, sport?"

"From the house over there. See?" Caleb pointed to the cottage.

"Can you sit up, sir?" Tess asked.

"Course I can. Just don't want to."

"I'm afraid you have to." Again Tess kept her voice gentle, and she smiled at the sick man. It must have been something in the smile she gave him, or maybe her tone of voice, that made him immediately try to sit up. Luke reached a strong hand to help, but Dave shrugged it off.

"I got this, boy," he wheezed. But even though he tried, he couldn't push himself up on his own. Luke and Tess helped him and then Luke stood and pulled Caleb away as Tess opened her bag and reached for a bottle of baby aspirin. Taking four out, she handed them to him and he put them in his mouth.

"Don't swallow them. They work faster if you chew," she advised.

"How'd ya know it was my ticker?" he asked, as he put a hand to his chest.

"Caleb told me you had heart problems. I'm going to listen to it now, if you'll let me." Tess had taken out a stethoscope and was warming it with the palm of her hand.

"Guess so. But don't do nothin' invasive, if ya know what I mean."

She was concerned at the way he had to work hard to catch his breath. "Nothing invasive, promise. How long have you been in pain?" She put the instrument on his chest, listening to the intermittent beats. Not strong. Hopefully, the aspirin was working to lessen any blockage.

"'Bout two hours, I guess. Started right after I spoke with Barrett this afternoon."

She turned to glance at Luke and he just shook his head. Sarah, she noticed, was clutching Luke's arm as though it was a life preserver. The woman looked worried, and maybe just a hint guilty, but her face shifted into a neutral expression when she caught Tess looking.

Shaking her head, Tess turned back to her patient. "Try to keep quiet now. Help will be here soon," she soothed as she sat down next to him. "I have to keep you sitting up till they get here."

"Don't want no help. Don't like doctors. Not even non-doctors, or whatever you are. You're a pretty thing, though," he said, focusing on her face. Tess smiled.

"She looks like Grammy in the picture you showed me from when she was young." Caleb kept hold of his grandfather's hand as he spoke.

"I'll be. That she does, sport." With that the older man closed his eyes for a minute.

Tess spied a single tear roll down his weathered, stubbly cheek. She turned to glance at Luke and caught a warm smile slanting across his handsome face. She quickly turned away. She didn't want to smile back at him. She was hurt and a little angry at him, still. He hadn't really said anything since they had gotten to the older man, just helped when he was needed. He had spoken briefly, in a low voice to Sarah, but Tess couldn't make out what he was saying.

What was taking the emergency crew so long? She cast a worried look at Caleb's grandfather, noting that his eyes were still closed and his breathing was shallow. It had been—she looked at her watch—fifteen minutes.

The sound of a sharp siren cut into her thoughts and she looked up to see Joe Mason pulling into the drive. He jumped out of the police vehicle and hurried over to the scene.

"I heard it on the scanner," he explained. "The medics are right behind me. I had to show them where the cottage was. Rural address and all. Thought it would be quicker."

Tess nodded and rubbed Dave's right shoulder. She heaved a sigh of relief as the emergency vehicle arrived on scene. She gave them Dave's vital signs and told them she had given him aspirin, as they took over. Then she stood aside and let them work.

"Good thing you were around, Tess." Joe put his hand on her shoulder as he spoke.

"Not me, Joe. Caleb is the hero here. He saw his grandfather from the upstairs porch and alerted us."

"Good job, young man!" Joe praised the boy.

Caleb blushed a little as his dad put his arm around his shoulders and gave him a hug.

"I'm not goin' nowhere with y'all!"

The old man's voice was weak but firm as he spoke to the paramedics. They looked over at Tess. Well, she was the senior medical person on scene, she reasoned to herself.

She walked over to the stretcher and took Dave's hand, feeling compassion swell within her.

"I know how you feel. I wouldn't want to go, either, but you have to. You have too many people who care about you, and want you to be around awhile longer. Think of Caleb, sir. You have to let these men help you so you can get better, for your grandson's sake. I'd like to visit with you after you get checked out, if that's okay?"

The old man took a breath and leaned back against the padded stretcher. Whatever fight was left in him seemed to suddenly drain away as he looked up at her.

"I'd like that, girl. I really would," he whispered.

"Then it's a deal. I'd really like that, too." Tess leaned down and kissed his forehead and then motioned for the paramedics to get him to the ambulance. She knew it would be touch and go for the man for some time.

Luke, Caleb and Sarah walked next to Dave and reassured him that everything would be all right. At one point Luke looked back at Tess over his shoulder. He was smiling that smile that always caused her stomach to end up somewhere in the region of her throat. He mouthed the words *thank you* before bending down to say something in Caleb's ear. The boy nodded and turned back to wave at her. She waved back, then wrapped her arms around herself in a protective gesture.

She had done it. She had managed to perform medically without freezing. She was elated, yet confused. She also felt drained. She just wanted to go home, and maybe not to the cottage. Maybe back to Seattle. Although the cottage seemed more homey and this town more real and welcoming right now than Seattle did. Tess felt another wave of confusion. She really did have some thinking to do.

Why hadn't Luke told her?

Chapter Twelve

"So, you were here when I called you." It was a statement, not a question.

Luke was sitting in his former father-in-law's hospital room, gazing at the man lying in the bed. Three days after his collapse, Dave was doing much better. Fortunately, the heart attack had been a minor one, and Tess had done all the right things to keep it from worsening.

Katherine had flown in right away and taken charge of her irascible husband. It seemed that no one else could deal with him, especially the hospital staff. He was rude to everyone. Everyone except Caleb. Katherine was the only one who could keep him in line, and amazingly, he became almost docile when she was around. She and Caleb had left earlier to go shopping for school clothes.

To say that Luke was shocked that Dave had shown up in the village was an understatement. He didn't mind the man coming, but a little notice would have been nice.

"Yeah, I was here. Thanks to the lovely Miss Fulcher, who picked me up from the airport."

"I wish you had told me you were coming, but I'm glad you're here. We have some things to discuss and it's good to do it face-to-face." Luke picked up his coffee from the night table and took a long drink. He had asked the doctors if Dave was up for the conversation and they had agreed, as long as he didn't get riled up.

"Well, when Sarah told me about that woman, what else could I do? My grandson is the most important person in our lives. Katherine and I want what's best for him."

"I'm fairly certain that your information about 'that woman' is inaccurate, but your concerns are valid. You love your grandson, and I'm grateful that you do. Family is important. But I want you to understand that I love my son more than life. I would never put him in harm's way."

"I believe that you do love him," the old man conceded gruffly, "but you've never been a father." He held up his hand as Luke began to speak, effectively stopping him. "I'm not saying that you would deliberately put him in danger. Just saying that you have to be careful with your kids, especially these days."

Luke's tone was matter-of-fact as he answered. Best to just put it out there and be honest with the man. "Tess does have PTSD, but as someone who's suffered from the same condition in the past, I assure you that she is working hard to get through it and get her life back on track. She's been through therapy. That's why she came here, for a fresh start in a peaceful place where she could take the time to put the pieces back together. She's not a dangerous person. In fact, quite the opposite. She's kind, compassionate, giving and loving."

As for Sarah, since the incident at Moon Gate Cottage, Luke had found it difficult to be more than superficially polite to her. He said a silent prayer that God would see fit to insert a little compassion into Sarah's heart. He knew it was there, just not for Tess. He also knew that Sarah liked him, and he liked her, despite her breach of trust in sharing false information with Caleb's grandparents. But he didn't love her in the way that she wanted him to. He hadn't realized how much she wanted it until she had shown up at the cottage with Dave Lockard in tow. Luke had been blind to the depth of her feelings and felt badly about it. She'd behaved cruelly, but she'd been desperate not to lose him—even though she'd never really had him. The fault was partially his for not straightening her out sooner. As for the other woman in his life, Tess…

He more than liked Tess, but he doubted that she wanted to have anything to do with him now that she knew he had hidden the fact that he had been with her on that day in Afghanistan The look on her face had said it all.

"Humph. That's the way you see it. Although she was good when she tended to me the other day. Capable, for one thing. Not like these idiots here. She…wasn't what I'd expected from what the other lady said." Dave cleared his throat before adding, "Caleb, his grandmother and I had a long talk this morning."

Luke nodded. "Good, I'm glad. I wanted to give you time alone with him."

"Well, I've got to tell you, his grandmother and I are still ready to take him," Dave said gruffly. "But it seems that he loves you and wants to stay with you. The courts will take that into consideration, and we're well aware of it." The older man rubbed his eyes tiredly. "Look, Barrett, we only want what's best for the boy."

Luke caught the slight pleading note in the man's voice and felt compassion. All this angst over the love for a child. They both had the same goal.

"I only want what's best for him, as well. You and Katherine are wonderful grandparents, but I'm his father. And new as I am to that, I take the job very seriously. I've never loved anyone the way I love that kid."

"You know that we tried to get custody when Jennifer moved out of the house. We didn't think she'd be able to handle being a single parent. I guess we should have had more faith in her. I don't know. We didn't want her to go, but she got a good job after the baby was born, and wanted to be out on her own again. The house was so empty when they left. I thought if we could get custody of the boy, then she would come home."

He shook his head. His eyes had a faraway look as he remembered things that Luke had no knowledge of, so he let him talk without interrupting.

"Then she got sick, and we tried again, because she refused to come home and let us take care of her. Don't know why I'm telling you all of this," the older man said abruptly. "The past doesn't matter. Caleb's future is my real concern."

"We'll work it out, Dave," Luke said simply. And he meant it. He hadn't had to tell Caleb anything. The boy's grandfather had taken care of that, and evidently Caleb had given him an answer that he had reluctantly accepted.

"We can give him so much. When Jennifer married you, I thought that she was marrying beneath her. You had nothing and were a young pup in the military. What kind of a life could you give her? I was thrilled when she left you to come home. Validation of what I had told her all along. I suppose you think that was just me being a cantankerous old windbag. That's what Katherine says. She was always on your side."

"No. You were being a good father and grandfather, trying to do your very best for your daughter and grandson. In your heart, you were doing the right thing for both of them. Don't ever doubt that. I don't."

Luke felt a lump form in his throat as he thought of the love this man had for his family. It was a love worth fighting for with every fiber of his being. Dave's decisions may not have been the right ones, but *he* felt they were and that was what had kept him fighting. Luke knew that his own willingness to fight to keep his son was born of a love like no other, and this man lying in the hospital bed was proof positive of that. You fight for the people you hold close in your heart. God puts you where you were meant to be, whether you want to be there or not.

"Now it's my turn to do what's best for my family," Luke continued. "And Tess is part of that. I don't know if you can see it or not, but she really has been good for

Caleb and for me. She's a good woman, Dave. I would never leave Caleb with her if she wasn't."

"I hear she's a physician assistant? She helped save my life."

"She is and she did. Had a rough time when she volunteered to go to Afghanistan with a medical organization, but she's working through it."

"Pretty little thing," Dave said. "I saw the way you looked at her, too. You might want to think of courting that one. Just a thought. Caleb is certainly taken with her. I hear she throws a mean softball."

Luke glanced up in surprise. The way he looked at Tess? How did he look at Tess?

You look at her like you just might be interested in her.

This time he didn't push the thought away. *Who says you can't be interested in a woman and raise a son at the same time?*

Well, I said it, he mused. *But it's possible I may have been wrong.*

"I'll give it some thought," Luke said with a wide grin. Courting Tess appealed to him. The more he allowed himself to think about it, the more he liked the idea. But first, he needed to talk to her. Explain why he hadn't told her about Afghanistan. Hopefully, being the Tess that he thought he knew, she would listen and understand.

From my lips to Your ears, Lord, he prayed silently.

Tess tried to pull into the driveway at the cottage but there wasn't room. Three delivery trucks were parked in a straight line, one after the other. Men from one truck were busy unloading what looked like an inordinate number of white wooden chairs, along with white wooden tables.

Another truck with a party supply logo on the side had a different group of men working from it, carrying white tents through the moon gate into the backyard. Miss Annie was standing next to the third truck, which sported a local catering company's sign. She waved cheerily and blew Tess a kiss before turning back to the group of ladies she was conversing with.

Tess turned around and drove to the rear of the house, where Katie was standing with a clipboard and barking orders on placement of the items. A drill sergeant had nothing on her, Tess thought, shaking her head.

"Tess, dear, don't park on the grass, please. Stay on the dirt path," Katie shouted over to her when she saw the compact car.

It was setup day for the luncheon, and Tess had to admit that it looked like a three-ring circus at the cottage. She had stepped out to get her hair cut, at the aunts' invitation, while the preparations for the luncheon were going on. The sisters had made an appointment for her at the only salon in town, a treat, they said, for helping Luke with Caleb. Tess had protested that it wasn't necessary, but Aunt Annie had shushed her, saying that it was a small thing and everyone loved going to the beauty salon once in a while. It was a nice girlie thing to do. She had to admit it felt good to be pampered a bit, and had ended with a French manicure and pedicure along with the haircut.

She got out if the car and approached Aunt Katie. It was time to tell them that she was thinking of leaving Swansboro. She hated the thought, but she had made the decision that it might be time. She had feelings for Luke, but they were conflicted and confusing—a mix of attraction and anger. He made her feel safe, while at the same time she wondered if she could even trust him after the secret he'd kept from her for all this time.

She'd come to Swansboro to get away from the real world while she recovered...but now she needed to get away from Swansboro while she regrouped and dealt with the tangled mess of emotions Luke made her feel. Maybe it was best that she go back to Seattle.

But you have obligations here, she reminded herself. *You've never shirked a commitment in your life. What about the cakewalk and, more importantly, taking care of Caleb?*

You can't leave yet. Not until Luke finds a replacement for you. You promised him. She shook her head. She hated it when she was right. She sighed and promised herself she would leave once the church festival was over and Luke had found a responsible person to take care of his son. Caleb had spent the rest of the week with his grandparents and Luke, and she hadn't seen any of them since the day Dave Lockard had collapsed.

"Hey, Aunt Katie." She leaned to kiss the softly wrinkled cheek that the older lady proffered before she began shouting at several workmen who were carrying a load of chairs.

"Snap to it, gentlemen. I don't have all day!"

"Wow. Looks like you all have been busy."

"You don't know the half of it, dear. We still have linens to be delivered. Annie is setting up a schedule with the catering people right now. I hope she gets the times correct. I just know I'll have to go behind her and make sure."

"Do you have a couple of minutes?"

"Absolutely! Annie and I have been waiting for you to get back. Hang on a second." With that she reached into her pocket, pulled out a walkie-talkie and clicked the button smartly before speaking into it. "Butterfly, this is Hummingbird. Come in, Butterfly."

There was a slight pause and then a crackle came over the handset as Annie answered. Tess raised her hand to cover her mouth as she pretended to cough in order to conceal a laugh.

"Sister? Is that you?"

Katie rolled her eyes. "Of course it's me. Who else would have the other walkie-talkie? And call me Hummingbird. We agreed that Hummingbird and Butterfly would be our code names."

Another crackle and then Annie spoke again. "Oh, right. Yes, Hummingbird?"

"Meet us in the house. Juliet wants to discuss something with us. *Your code name,*" she mouthed to Tess.

"Of course," Tess murmured, so wanting to laugh.

Crackle, crackle, and Annie spoke once more. "On my way, Hummingbird. Stat."

Tess took Katie's hand, leading her toward the cottage, but the woman stopped in midstride and turned to look back at the people working in the yard and garden.

"I'll be back shortly. Carry on, and remember I can

see you from the windows." Her voice was friendly, but had a distinctly firm edge as she gestured toward the cottage.

A few minutes later the three of them were seated at the old oak table in the sunny kitchen, with frosty glasses of iced tea. Tess looked at the women and smiled. Aunt Katie had the clipboard in front of her. Aunt Annie held Jack in her arms and was telling her what a beautiful puppy she was. Tess rubbed her finger around the rim of her glass in a slightly nervous gesture that the aunts had not picked up on. Or so she thought.

"Tess, are you all right?" Katie was giving her an assessing look over the rims of her glasses.

"Well, since you ask, no, I'm not." Tess felt her face heating a little as she answered.

"Oh, dear. I'm so sorry. Is it your leg? I thought it was getting better. Are you in pain? Would you like a BC Powder?" Annie gave Tess an empathetic look as she reached over to touch her hand.

"Oh, no, Auntie, my leg is fine. Much better, in fact. I rarely use the cane anymore."

"If it's about all of the organized chaos going on right now—" Katie waved a hand in the air dismissively "—it just looks that way because everyone is here at once. They'll be gone soon," she assured her.

"Oh, no. It's not that at all. I… It's time for me to go back to Seattle, I think." There. It was out and she felt like crying.

"Oh, no, dear. You can't leave. Not now." The stunned look on Annie's face was almost Tess's undoing. She didn't want to leave, but she had to. How could she explain it to them and have it make sense? She wasn't sure it made sense to her. She had come to love these two incredible ladies in such a short period of time, not to mention the town and its funny, lovely inhabitants.

"Nonsense!" Katie stated roundly. "You can't leave. You are committed to helping at the Summer Fest at the church. You're also committed to caring for Caleb. One doesn't walk out on commitments, now, does one, dear? What brought this on, if I might ask?"

"Oh, I'll not leave until after the festival. And before I go, I'll make sure Luke finds someone to care for Caleb. I wouldn't leave everyone in the lurch. But after those situations are taken care of…well, I think it's time."

Tess hadn't planned to tell them about finding out that Luke had saved her life in Afghanistan, but the story came out, anyway. She couldn't have stopped herself if she had wanted to, and she *had* wanted to keep it to herself. But when she began, and saw the sympathetic looks on their face and felt the pure love radiating toward her, she kept going until it was all out, sitting on the table between them for inspection and deciphering. For that's exactly what they did.

"I always knew that Luke was a hero. And my, it really is a small world. What are the odds?" Annie sighed dreamily. "Oh, dear, you are so blessed that he was there."

"Yes, sister, she certainly is. And since I doubt you're angry with him for saving you, I'd guess you're upset that he didn't mention it once he saw you again?"

Tess nodded in agreement.

"Seems to me he didn't out of kindness and respect for you," Katie continued. "Why are you angry, dear?"

Tess sighed. "That's just it, I don't know. I guess I feel like if I had known up front, it might have helped me sooner…maybe. Oh, I don't know. It just feels like he lied."

"It wasn't a lie. He just didn't say anything. I think, instead of running away, you need to face him and ask him why he omitted that bit of information."

"But isn't that a lie by omission?"

"Not at all, my dear. I know Luke Barrett, and believe me, sooner or later he would have told you. He would never have kept it to himself. He knows what you've been going through, trying to come to terms with what happened. He was probably just trying to give you time to work things out before he spoke up." Annie rubbed Tess's arm tenderly as she spoke.

"She's right." Katie reached over and took Tess's free hand before adding, "You can't keep running from your problems, Tess. This is a good life God has given us. Live it! I can't emphasize that enough. You are blessed in so many ways. Why can't you see it?" The last was said gently and with love.

Tess felt her eyes tear up. They were right. She had learned so much and gotten so much from the people in this town in the short time she had been here. They had helped her heal in ways she couldn't begin to describe. She loved this village and had really thought she wanted to stay and make a home here. Livie had given her a gift when she had sent her here.

Did it really matter that Luke hadn't said anything? Was she just looking for a reason to slip back into her old pity party for one? And as far as Luke went, she really liked him, more than a little. *But no, what man in his right mind would want a woman with so much baggage?*

She hadn't realized she had spoken aloud until she heard Annie chuckle.

"I see now," the woman said. "Honey, you don't have half the baggage you think you do. Not really any more than the rest of us. Talk to him. I suspect you might be surprised. Sister and I think that he might like you more than a little, too." She looked at her twin, who nodded in agreement.

"He's a good man, Tess. I think he might want to talk this out with you, knowing Luke as I do. And I know him well." Katie jumped to her feet. "Now that that's sorted out, we have work to do! Can't leave these people alone for too long. Come, Butterfly, and don't forget your walkie-talkie."

With that, the aunts were gone, Annie giggling as they walked out of the door. Tess couldn't hear what they were saying, but she had a sneaking suspicion it had to do with her and Luke.

She would talk to him. She owed him that much. He had saved her life, literally. Aunt Annie was right; it was a small world. What were the odds that she would end up in the same place as the marine?

Chapter Thirteen

Tess woke early on the Saturday morning of the luncheon and headed for the small sun-bleached wooden dock at the edge of the backyard, pausing momentarily to look at the decorations. They really were beautiful, she thought. So simple, yet elegant.

She had to admit that the garden provided a perfect backdrop for the affair. All the flowers were in glorious multicolored bloom. The trellis was heavy with fragrant, old-fashioned roses.

Shaking her head to clear her thoughts, Tess moved on to the dock. She wanted to get a quick swim in. She needed the warmth and healing of Bogue Sound this morning before everyone descended on the cottage.

Gracefully, she slid into the water and began a casual backstroke as she stared unseeingly at the pink clouds that drifted through the early morning sky. The warmth of the sea enveloped her and she let out a small grateful sigh. This was therapy at its finest and she desperately needed the tranquillity it always brought her.

Turning over, she brought her legs together and gave a perfect mermaid flip to propel her back toward the dock. Thankfully, her leg was much stronger.

She reached the dock and had raised her arms to pull herself up when a much larger hand came into view, offering her help. Looking up, she saw Luke standing at the edge, grinning down at her. She put her hand in his and he lifted her out of the water as if she weighed no more than a baby.

"What are you doing here? The ladies will be arriving soon," she warned him as she reached for her towel. She felt vulnerable standing in front of him in her one-piece bathing suit, conscious of the scar on her leg. He looked as handsome as ever, that grin slanting across his firm lips.

"Thought it would be a good time to talk to you. I didn't want to put it off any longer."

"Okay. I'm listening." Tess wrapped a towel around herself and shivered slightly. She felt a little off balance at his unexpected appearance. Taking a deep breath, she looked past him to the garden.

"Not here. Let's go to the house." Was it her imagination, or did he seem nervous, as well?

"Where is Caleb?" she asked as they took seats at the table on the patio.

"With his grandparents. Dave should be released tomorrow. Thank you for what you did. You saved his life, according to the doctors, by giving him the aspirin."

"I really didn't do anything." Tess felt her cheeks warm and changed the subject. "Did you get the custody problem straightened out?"

She really wanted to know. The issue had weighed so heavily on Luke's mind. Her heart had ached for him. She sincerely hoped everything had been settled. He didn't look as tired today as he had the last time she had seen him. His mood seemed lighter and she was glad of that. It really did bother her to see him bearing the weight of the world, for that was what it truly must have felt like.

"We came to an understanding. Caleb will stay here. He told his grandfather that he didn't want to leave. Dave and I have bonded a little over our mutual love for Caleb. It's a cautious truce, but it's a beginning."

"Oh, Luke, I'm so glad." She unwittingly reached for his hand as she spoke, giving it a soft squeeze, then jerked away as she realized what she had done. His skin felt like strong smooth red-hot steel, leaving a burning imprint behind. Surprisingly, he reached for her withdrawn hand and enveloped it in his own, his azure eyes darkening as he looked into hers. Her heart skipped a beat and she could feel a blush developing, but she didn't try to pull away. It felt right, having her hand securely clasped in his, and at the realization her confusion deepened.

"Tess, I am very sorry that I didn't tell you about being with you at the orphanage. I just felt that it would somehow make things worse for you, by awakening memories you were trying so hard to forget." He turned his head and looked at the calm blue water intently.

She studied his profile closely and began to feel guilty. She was struck by the sincerity etched on his face and the doubt in his eyes, doubt that plainly told her he questioned the decision he'd made, even though he'd done it for her sake. It wasn't that he wasn't concerned, she realized. She didn't need a map to read the trepidation she glimpsed in those eyes. It was there plain as day.

The look pulled at her heart, and she wanted nothing more than to reassure him. Her anger dissolved. He truly thought that he had done the right thing in not telling her.

But she still had questions. Questions that had been gnawing at her since she had learned that he was the marine who had carried her down the mountain. Questions that she felt would help her deal with what had happened. She gently pulled her hand out of his and took a breath.

"Luke, I was angry at you for not telling me sooner," she admitted. "I kept wondering why you seemed so familiar, why your voice struck a chord, even if your face didn't. I heard your voice in my dreams every night, telling me that you would take care of me, make sure I was safe. I carried it with me for months. I'm not sure how I didn't connect the dots."

"I recognized you the moment I saw you sleeping in the living room," Luke murmured. "And when I believed you recognized me that day at church, I thought we could talk after breakfast. Then I realized you really didn't know who I was. I promise you that I was going to say something at some point, after you seemed to be coming to terms with everything. I can see now that I was wrong to wait. Forgive me, Tess."

"Did anyone else survive?" Tess blurted out the

words abruptly. She had to know. She had been wondering for months. The hope that not all the children
had perished had kept her from going quietly insane
with grief.

"Yes, Tess, there were plenty of children and adults
who did make it through the carnage of that horrific
day." His words were strong and low, and Tess sighed
with relief. Tears pricked the backs of her eyes and she
uttered a soft prayer.

"Thank You, God. Oh, God, thank You for keeping them safe."

And though her heart still ached for the children
who had been lost, the news that she had not been the
only survivor was music to her ears. She felt as though
a millstone had been lifted from her soul. She knew
that the other two in her medical team of three had not
made it, and that the child she had been holding when
the explosion occurred had not survived, but that was
all she had known for certain.

The smile Tess gave him was genuine and lit her
beautiful face. Luke felt as if he had been punched in the
gut. She was gorgeous sitting there with her hair wet, a
sprinkle of freckles scattered across her pert nose and
soft cheeks, the towel wrapped around her modestly.
Her beauty, from within and without, was refreshing.
He almost forgot what he was going to say and had to
collect his thoughts.

"Is there anything else you want to know that you
don't remember?"

"What you've told me is so much more than I could

ever have hoped to know. That question has been with me for months. I had assumed that no one else made it except me." She frowned as she said the last words, then shook her head as if to clear thoughts that no longer need haunt her waking moments and dreams. It seemed to be enough for now, and he wished with all his being that he had talked to her about this long ago. If only he had known how much it would have helped her and not hurt her. Hindsight was twenty-twenty.

"If you ever want to talk about it more, I'm always here for you. Always, Tess."

"I know that I will. Thank you, Luke, but what you've told me is enough for now."

He cleared his throat, because his voice sounded gruff to his ears. Yes, he would always be there for her—he knew that in his heart. He wanted nothing more in life than to be there for his son and Tess. Suddenly he felt like an awkward schoolboy getting ready to ask a girl out for the first time. Since when did he get nervous? He was a battle-hardened marine. They didn't get nervous.

"Thank you, Luke, for everything, but most of all for saving my life. I really thought that God had made a mistake by keeping me alive and letting so many innocent people die. But He brought me here and showed me through all of you that life is still good and meant to be lived. It's such a glorious gift." She hesitated before adding with conviction and strength, "I'll never take a moment for granted again. Ever."

He nodded. "I'd do the same a thousand more times

for you if you needed it." Well, that sounded awkward and ridiculous, but she only smiled softly at the words.

"Which leads me to another issue we need to discuss." Again that nervous feeling washed over him; nerves and a bit of excitement mixed. "I hear that you're thinking of leaving soon."

He watched her face closely. She looked dumbfounded before clarity lit her jade eyes as she nodded. "The aunts?"

"The aunts," he confirmed. "They told me when I went to speak to them last evening. I thought you loved this place as much as I did? Why would you want to leave? I know Seattle is a nice city, but it's got nothing on Swansboro." He tried to sound calm and casual, but the thought of her leaving had taken all of the wind out of his sails for a moment. He needed to convince her to stay; if he could.

Lord, please help me to convince her that this was all as You meant it to be. You brought her back into my life for a reason. She was meant to be with Caleb and me. She was meant to make this village her home.

"Luke, I love this town and wish that I could stay, but it's time to go back to the real world. But not until you've found someone to care for Caleb," she added hurriedly. "I would never leave you in the lurch." Her words gave him hope that he had at least a little bit of time left to change her mind.

"What will you do?" he asked curiously, his heart still contracting a bit at the thought that she would leave the village and he might never see her again.

"I don't know. I really haven't thought it all the way through. With what you've told me today, and being able to help Mr. Lockard, I'm sure I can go back to work now. I'll get a job and pick up the pieces and move on, I suppose."

"Why not stay, Tess? You have family here. Your brother lives three hours away. The aunts are here. You can get a job at the clinic. They're still looking for help. You have a church family that's taken you into their hearts, whether you wanted them to or not. Pick up the pieces here. You've already started. Finish."

He laughed a little as she rolled her eyes. She had fought tooth and nail to not get involved, but the town refused to let her withdraw. It had been a conspiracy of sorts, but a lovely one filled with good intentions. From the moment she had hit town, the villagers had done their best to help her move beyond the tragedy that had dogged her for months.

"I want to," she whispered, doubt in her eyes.

He cleared his throat again. There was no way to say what he had to say next other than to, well, just say it. If she said no, so be it. He knew that just as his son was worth fighting for, so was this woman.

"I want you to stay, Tess. Caleb wants you to stay."

"You do? Both of you?"

"We do," he said with more confidence. "Especially me. I want you to stay so that we can get better acquainted. I want to court you, if you'll let me, that is. I have permission from the aunts," he added quickly when he saw the look on her face.

"You do?" she asked faintly.

"Yes. I asked them last night. It's why I went to see them. Please say yes."

Court. Such a lovely old-fashioned word. Such a lovely word, period. Suddenly the clouds in Tess's heart and mind began to clear and the sun shone a little brighter, if that was possible. Luke wanted to court her, baggage and all! The words swirled through her mind and tangled with her emotions.

"Yes, please." It was all she could think of to say. It was the only thing she wanted to say.

Luke crossed the distance between them and lifted her gently, wet towel and all, into his strong arms. She felt at home there, instinctively remembering from her dreams the safe embrace of the day he had saved her life. He kissed her gently on her forehead. She closed her eyes and laid her head under his chin, breathing a simple prayer of thanks to God. All things *were* possible with God and she thanked Him a thousand times for bringing Luke back into her life once more.

As he sat down in the chair with her in his arms, a thought occurred to her.

"Luke, what will people say? It seems so fast. What about Sarah?"

"It's not so fast. I've known you for almost a year, and really, for my whole life. I've been waiting for you forever. As for Sarah, she's a friend. Nothing more, nothing less. As for what people think, who cares?" She started to say something, but he lifted a finger and pressed it to her lips. "Seriously, who cares?" he whispered quietly.

She stared into his eyes and couldn't quite think of a reason she should care what anyone else thought. Everything that had been on her mind was forgotten as she felt herself caught up in his serious gaze. Her lips tingled where his finger touched them lightly, and his words warmed her.

"You're right." Then another thought occurred to her. "What about Caleb? Will he be all right with this?"

"Are you serious? That kid thinks you're the best thing since the Cardinals won the World Series. Caleb will be thrilled." Luke gave her that slow, easy smile and her heart tripped.

"And I think he is, too."

Luke looked intently into her eyes. Then he leaned forward and kissed her gently on her mouth. It was a prayer and a vow wrapped in one exquisite gesture, and Tess felt her heart melt. She felt him sigh as he pulled back and she laid her head on his shoulder, watching seabirds dip and dive in the distance over the sound.

"I want to ask you something before we talk about other things. So many other things." His voice was low and gruff as it rumbled close to her ear. She peered up and caught the serious look on his handsome face.

"Okay. What is it?" She pulled back and put a hand on his cheek. He closed his eyes for a moment and then drew her hand to his mouth to kiss the palm gently.

"Are you okay with attending church with Caleb and me? Are you still struggling with your faith?"

The look in his beautiful eyes was so intense. Tess

realized that this was a very important matter to him. He was a man of strong faith. He lived it daily and made certain that his son knew God, as well. Her whole life prior to the bombing had been predicated on faith and her love of God. She had become lost for a while, but knew that she was making her way back to Him. The anger was gone and had been replaced by hope.

She smiled at Luke gently and stroked her hand over his cheek. "Of course I'll attend services with you and Caleb. The anger is gone, Luke. I may not have the answers I was looking for, but I have faith now that He had a plan. I just happened to be an unwilling witness to it. But I know now in my heart that I was there for a reason, and so were you. No struggles on my part any longer. It was His will. I'm making my way home."

The light that shone in Luke's eyes almost took her breath away, and she caught it again when he leaned forward and kissed her gently, framing her face with his strong hands.

"He brought me you not once, but twice. How blessed I am," Luke said softly against her lips. Tess's heart melted at his words. Then a thought struck her.

"Oh, the time!" She stood up, reluctant to leave the safe haven of his arms. "The aunts will be here soon. I have to shower and get dressed or I'll be sitting at the luncheon in a wet bathing suit."

He gave a disappointed pout before giving her that wonderful smile, and her heart skipped a beat. She hoped that feeling never went away, and she promised herself that she would never let it, although she had a pretty good idea she wouldn't have to try too hard.

Had there ever been a better day? she wondered. Had God ever given her so much at once? Again she sent a heartfelt prayer heavenward. Life was so good. Let the courtship begin.

Epilogue

"**B**utterfly, this is Hummingbird. Come in, Butterfly."
Katie Salter held the walkie-talkie close to her mouth as
she tried to get her sister to answer. No response. "Butterfly, are you there?" No response.

"Maybe she put it down somewhere," Luke suggested, when he saw the look of consternation on Miss
Katie's face.

"Well, she had better pick it up. I've got a bride ready
to walk down the aisle. Where could my sister be?"

"We'll go look if you want us to, Aunt Hummingbird." Little Annie piped up, and her twin sister nodded
her bright red head in agreement.

"Aunt *Katie*, dear, and yes—please go see if you can
find her. And don't get your dresses dirty." Katie looked
down at her great-grandniece with a pained look on her
face. Clearly the moniker Aunt Hummingbird didn't sit
well with her, even from a six-year-old. *Ah well*, Luke
thought. *Terms of endearment.*

"I like Aunt Hummingbird better," the little girl said pertly, before she raced off in the direction of the backyard.

"So do I," Luke heard little Katie assure her sister as they ran past him.

"Relax, Miss Katie. Everything is beautiful and we have plenty of time," Luke assured the older woman with a smile.

His wedding day. He was in awe. A year ago if someone had told him that he would be getting married he would have laughed at them. He couldn't have imagined it happening. Today he couldn't imagine it not happening. He couldn't imagine life without Tess, and he didn't want to. It seemed that he had been waiting for her all his life and now she was here. Soon, the good Lord willing, they would have a family—brothers and sisters for Caleb. Tess would be a wonderful mother, and with God's help he would try his best each day to be a good father to his children.

"Luke, you'd better get out there. Tell Adam that he needs to be with you. Did you give Michael the ring? Where is Michael?" Miss Katie looked around the guest room as if searching for the two men.

"Aunt Katie, I gave him the ring, and he's already out by the rose trellis with Caleb and Adam."

Katie heaved a sigh and then shot Luke a critical look, her face softening slightly as she took in his appearance.

"I declare, child, you are so handsome, especially in those dress blues. And I like that you just called me Aunt Katie. Makes it official that in an hour you will be family for real." She cleared her throat and Luke could have sworn that he saw her eyes tear up. She really was a sweetheart. He walked over to her and took her in his arms, hugging her tightly.

"Love you, Auntie," he whispered above her head.

"Love you back, nephew." She cleared her throat again and pushed him away, patting his chest with both hands. "All righty, then. I really must find Annie and figure out what's going on out there. The natives are probably getting restless."

Just then, the walkie-talkie crackled and Miss Annie's voice could be heard asking for Hummingbird. Katie scooped up the handset and shot an exasperated look at Luke, while pointing to the door.

"Annie! Where have you been?"

"I've been here—well, mostly here, until Jack ran off with the walkie-talkie. The babies found it under one of the food tables in the buffet tent. So anyway, I thought I was Butterfly."

"You *are* Butterfly. Sheesh."

"What did you need? Oh…over. Am I supposed to say over?"

"No, you don't have to say over. Is everything in place? Is Reverend Fulcher ready?"

"Yeppers. You can send the bride out stat. Everyone has been seated… I think."

"What does that mean, you *think*?"

Katie sighed, shaking her head, and locked eyes again with a grinning Luke. A smile lit her face in return as she made hand motions, shooing him from the room. He walked out the door and headed for his place in front of the seated guests. He was more than ready.

* * *

"You look beautiful, girl. Are you nervous?" Livie asked. She helped her cousin Harper and Luke's sister, Molly, fluff the skirt of Tess's wedding dress one more time before putting her hands on Tess's shoulders and leaning in to kiss her cheeks.

"I hope Luke thinks so. No, not nervous, just anxious to get started on a new chapter in my life." Tess smiled at her sister-in-law and Harper before looking in the mirror.

"Well, if Hummingbird and Butterfly have their way, your day will be nothing short of perfect. And how could Luke not think you're beautiful, especially today? I suspect he thinks you're the best thing since colored jelly beans, anyway," Harper said stoutly as she adjusted Tess's fingertip wedding veil and small pearl tiara one more time. "Perfect," she pronounced softly. "Just so perfect. Too bad your parents couldn't be here."

Tess liked Livie's cousin Harper and Luke's sister, Molly. Harper and her children were getting ready to move back to Swansboro after a long absence. She was just as kind and loving as Livie, and Tess was happy to have her at the wedding.

As for Molly, she had welcomed Tess with open arms and an open heart, as had her husband, Sam. Luke's nieces and nephews were funny and warm. It was a big, wonderful family and she was happy that she was part of it now.

Turning to the mirror, she looked at herself thoughtfully one last time. She missed her parents and wished they could be there, but it couldn't be helped. Once again they were in the middle of nowhere in Africa and couldn't get out in time. Bless them both. The work they were doing as medical missionaries was important, but they promised a celebration when they returned. They couldn't wait to meet Luke and their new grandson.

"Come on, girls, it's time…" Katie poked her head in the door and her voice trailed away when she saw Tess. "Oh, my dear. You are stunning. Simply stunning. Words fail me." The older woman's face softened as she continued to stare at Tess. "You know, I think you are the most beautiful bride I have ever seen," she declared quietly.

Tess moved over to hug Aunt Katie. "Thank you," she whispered in her ear. "Thank you for everything."

The woman nodded before speaking. "Don't thank me yet, dear. Annie is out there and I have no idea what the seating looks like."

Livie and Tess laughed as they took Aunt Katie's arms and headed for the garden. Harper gave Tess a thumbs-up as she left to take her place in the audience, and Molly kissed her cheek.

Livie was Tess's matron of honor. Little Katie and Annie were doing double duty as flower girls and bridesmaids. Aunt Katie and Aunt Annie were giving the bride away. Adam, Caleb and Mike were Luke's groomsmen.

Mike was still adjusting to life after his injury. Just a week before the end of his deployment, he was injured by an improvised explosive device, leading to an amputation of his lower leg. Recovery had been a struggle, but the wedding had given him a goal to aim for—he'd been bound and determined to adjust to his prosthesis so he could stand by his best friend on Luke's wedding day.

To Tess's mind it was perfect. All family in the wedding party, which was exactly how she wanted it.

She looked over to a corner in the kitchen at her cane and smiled softly. She didn't need it any longer.

When they arrived at the French doors and stepped out, Tess could only smile and breathe a soft prayer of thanks to God. The day could not have been more perfect. It was late afternoon, that wonderful time before dusk. The weather was soft and warm, with a gentle breeze blowing in off the sound. The sky was a clear Carolina blue with only a few puffy clouds drifting through it. The flowers in the garden were still in full bloom and the scent of the old cream and lavender roses that hung from the trellis mingled with the fresh salt air.

More than a hundred people were seated in white wooden chairs on either side of the velvety green grass aisle. As Tess had come to know more people in the village, the aunts had increased the size of the invitation list considerably.

"Well, we can't leave certain people out," Aunt Katie has reasoned, and Tess had let them go. They had worked so hard to bring this day together and she loved them even more for all they had done.

"Ready?" Livie gave Tess's arm a squeeze as she motioned for her daughters to come over. The younger twins picked up two white wicker baskets from the table on the terrace. They had filled them with petals from the garden earlier in the day.

"More than ready," Tess said, as Aunt Annie came up and took one of her arms, and Aunt Katie the other.

"I declare, Tess, I am so proud of you. You are lovely." Annie breathed the words softly as the string quartet began playing Pachelbel's Canon in D. "Look at Luke, dear."

Tess glanced toward the trellis and caught her breath at the sight of him standing tall and proud in his dress blues. He was so ruggedly handsome that love mingled with pride in her.

So, marine, here we are, she thought. *And I couldn't love you more.*

She marveled at the look in his eyes. She saw love and felt it even from this far away, mirroring the love for him that filled her heart. It enveloped her as if she was being held in his strong arms.

The little twins, with their mother following close behind, made their way down the aisle, tossing flower petals left and right. They took the job seriously, to the point that several guests ended up with petals in their laps and on their feet. Tess heard Joey Mason yell "Hey," as the girls seemed to take particular delight in flinging petals in his direction, and Livie had to grab their little arms and steer them toward the end of the aisle. Their whispered protests carried back to Tess and she began to laugh, as did nearly all the guests.

Finally, Tess was standing next to Luke. He reached over and took her hand in his as her brother, Adam, winked at her and Caleb grinned. Reverend Fulcher asked who gave her in marriage, and the aunts answered proudly, "We do." They each kissed her cheek before settling in the front row.

"Dearly beloved, we are gathered together in the sight of God to join this man and woman in holy matrimony." Reverend Fulcher spoke loudly and clearly.

"Today is truly a glorious day the Lord hath made," he continued, "as today both of you are blessed with the greatest of all God's gifts—the gift of abiding love and devotion between a man and a woman. All present here today—and those present in heart—wish both of you all of the joy, happiness and success that the world has to offer. As you travel through life together I caution you to remember that the true measure of success is to be found in the love that you hold within your heart. I ask that you hold on to that key very tightly. According to the Bible, nothing is of more importance than love. God is love. It is love that brings you here today, uniting two hearts and two spirits. As your lives continue to interweave as one, remember that it is love that makes this a glorious union. It is love that will cause this union to endure."

Taking a small breath, he looked out at the assembled guests and smiled. "Luke and Tess have asked to read vows to each other that they have selected especially for the occasion of their marriage. Luke, will you begin?"

Luke nodded and took both of Tess's hands in his own.

"I take you, Tess, to be my wife, loving you now and as you grow and develop into all that God intends. I will love you when we are together and when we are apart. When our lives are at peace and when they are in turmoil. In times of rest and in times of work. I will honor your goals and dreams and help you to fulfill them. From the depths of my being, I will seek to be open and honest with you. I say these things believing that God is in the midst of them all and with us always."

Mike handed Luke a plain gold band that he slid onto Tess's waiting finger.

"Oh, how lovely!" Aunt Annie sighed from the front row, a tissue held to her eyes.

"Annie, shush." Katie nudged her sister sharply.

"Ouch!" At her disgruntled reply, several guests laughed aloud.

"Tess would now like to read her vows to Luke. I believe they are from the Book of Ruth."

Tess looked up into Luke's eyes as she spoke clearly and sweetly.

"Entreat me not to leave you, or to return from following after you, for where you go I will go, and where you stay I will stay. Your people will be my people, and your God will be my God. And where you die, I will die and there I will be buried. May the Lord do with me and more if anything but death parts you from me."

Livie handed her a gold band that matched the one Tess was now wearing, and she slid it onto Luke's finger.

"Now, unless anyone objects…" The reverend paused and glanced around at the guests, some of whom were peeking for the most part at Sarah, who in turn was looking at Luke and Tess with a terse smile fixed on her lovely face. "Very good, then." The pastor seemed relieved that his daughter hadn't said anything. Pushing his glasses up the bridge of his nose, he intoned solemnly, "I now pronounce you man and wife. You may kiss the bride."

Loud cheers erupted as Luke took Tess into his arms and kissed her soundly. The smaller pair of twins, who had been sitting with a box near them, looked at Aunt Annie, who nodded with a broad smile. They opened the lid of the box and hundreds of multicolored butterflies winged their way skyward, enveloping the bride and groom in a soft cocoon of flickering color. Tess laughed with delight and held a hand out to touch the beautiful insects.

I'm Mrs. Luke Barrett, she thought with wonder as she gazed up at him again, as if to make sure it all hadn't been a dream. She received a loving look in return as he took her hand and faced the crowd.

"Folks, thank you all for coming to help Tess, Caleb and me celebrate our special day. Each and every one of you holds a special place in our hearts. We truly thank God for putting you in our lives. Please enjoy the reception. Plenty of good food, drink and music are waiting for you all just fifty feet away. My bride and I will join you shortly."

The guests began to make their way to the large area set up for the reception as Luke led Tess and Caleb around the house to the ivy-covered moon gate. The legend, long life, prosperity, good luck. Happily-ever-after. Tess believed in them. She had found hers.

Great minds think alike, she thought as they stood together under the arch. She reached out and touched a curved portion, just as Luke raised his hand and touched the same section, above her hand. They were each silent for a moment before he scooped her up in his arms and carried her through the gate.

"You are now officially a moon gate bride," he said, looking into her eyes.

"And I am so happy to be one. You seem to make a habit of carrying me places," she said with a laugh.

"Darling, I'll always carry you, through good times and bad. You are my heart, my soul, the very breath that I take each day." His voice was low, his look earnest. She caught her breath at what she saw in his eyes. She had no doubt that he meant every word.

"Just love me, Luke. Just love me."

"My darling Tess, how could I not love you? It would be like asking the sun not to rise each morning and set each evening."

"Hey! You forgot me!" Caleb's blue eyes, so like his father's, were shining with laughter.

"Never in a million years," Tess said, as she and Luke walked back to him, each taking a hand and leading him through the moon gate.

"We hate to interrupt, but we wanted a minute alone with you three." Adam had come up behind the couple, joined by his wife, his daughters and the aunts.

"You're not interrupting at all," Tess said.

"The aunts and Liv wanted to give you your gift away from prying eyes."

"There's no need for a present. You all have done so much for us, we couldn't possibly expect anything else. Besides, our gift is that you are our family. What more could we ask for?" Tess looked at them all with love, and Luke nodded in agreement.

"She's right, brother," he said, addressing Adam.

"No, she is not right." Katie came forward with an envelope in one hand, her sister's elbow clasped in the other.

"Please accept this gift," Annie said. "It is what we want to give you, and we did think long and hard before we made the decision, so don't ask us if we did. Actually, it was Livie's idea and we agreed to it. It does, after all, belong to her. Or rather, it *did*."

Annie gazed at the newlyweds with such a serious expression that Tess became a little nervous. The aunt had never looked so intent. What could the gift be? Tess looked at Livie questioningly. Her sister-in-law just shrugged and smiled. Luke took the envelope and held it for a minute.

"Please open it. We have a reception to get back to and you have to change your clothes. We haven't got all day, dears." Katie tried to make her voice firm, but Tess noticed…was that a quiver of emotion?

"All right. Open it, Luke." Tess watched her husband's expression change from smiling, to surprised, then shocked, all within the space of a few seconds.

"No," he said firmly. "We cannot possibly accept this." He shook his head and tried to give the paper and envelope back to the aunts and Livie.

"You can and you will. You and Caleb need to get out of that rental house and into a real home." It was Annie's turn to be firm, before she added, "By the way, Luke, did I tell you how handsome you look in that uniform?" She gave him a dreamy smile that had the rest of the family laughing.

"Yes, ma'am, you sure did." He gave her a loving smile before getting back to the matter at hand. But Katie cut him off.

"Oh, pish. I for one don't have time to stand here and argue back and forth. Moon Gate Cottage is yours now. You both love it and it certainly loves you. Besides, you're doing us a favor. We don't have time to keep up with it and neither does Livie. It is hers to give, you know, and it was her idea. We have plenty of other cottages around here. We also have many obligations in this town. I'm running for mayor next election." Aunt Katie announced the last part with a calculated smile. "If Clyde Woods can run this town, a monkey can. Not to say that I'm a monkey, but, well…you know."

"Oh, Aunties and Liv…" Tess felt her eyes flood with tears. "I don't know what to say."

"Just say yes, so we can go eat, stat! I'm starved. It's time to carpe diem! Besides, you belong here. You're a moon gate bride now." Annie's brown eyes were filled with so much love as she looked at Tess and Luke.

"Thank you from our hearts," Tess whispered. Luke and she hugged both aunts, Livie, Adam and the girls. Everyone had tears in their eyes. "Oh, Livie, are you sure? You love this place so much."

"Positive. I love this place because it's home, not necessarily because of the cottage. As Aunt Katie said, there are plenty of places for us to stay when we come home."

"Just get changed and get to the reception. You have

guests waiting." Katie took control again and led everyone but Tess and Luke through the moon gate toward the joyful crowd.

As they watched the family go back to the party, Luke glanced down at Tess.

"I love this family, almost as much as I love you. We are truly home now, sweetheart." Tess heard him sigh with satisfaction as he steered her toward the house to change clothes.

"Luke?"

"Hmm?"

"Will Mike be all right?"

"You have such a soft heart, Tess. Worried about him, are you?"

"Yes, I am. I know what it feels like to be wounded in a war zone."

"We'll make sure he's all right. He's a strong man, my love. We've known each other for years, and have lived together for the last three. He's home now, here at our wedding, celebrating with us."

Tess nodded, still concerned for the wounded warrior who was Luke's best friend.

"Luke?"

"Yes, love?"

"We need to teach Aunt Annie some different slang words."

"Agreed. We'll tackle that next week. For now, let's go celebrate this wonderful life that God has given us."

"Okay. I've never felt so blessed."

"Neither have I, my love. Neither have I."

With those words they walked into the cottage, eager

to begin sharing their lives. *God is everywhere*, Tess thought contentedly.

"Luke?"

"Hmm?"

"I love you."

"And I love you."

* * * * *

Dear Reader,

Love at times comes gently and when you least expect it. This book is about love, kindness, compassion, home and finding faith again, faith that I suspect was never *really* lost in the first place, just misplaced along the way.

I hope that you enjoyed and fell in love with the village of Swansboro and the lovely people who live there. I am blessed to be exceedingly familiar with this small town in coastal North Carolina, and want to share it with my readers. I also hope that you enjoyed Luke's and Tess's journey to their happily-ever-after and that you came to care for them as I do. I truly believe that God puts you where you were meant to be, as He did them, with each other and in the quaint hamlet they ended up calling home.

Thank you for reading my story. I would love to hear from you. You can email me at *rozldunbar@gmail.com*.

I wish for each of you peace and God's blessings.
Roz Dunbar

REQUEST YOUR FREE BOOKS!

2 FREE INSPIRATIONAL NOVELS
PLUS 2
FREE
MYSTERY GIFTS

Love Inspired®

YES! Please send me 2 FREE Love Inspired® novels and my 2 FREE mystery gifts (gifts are worth about $10). After receiving them, if I don't wish to receive any more books, I can return the shipping statement marked "cancel." If I don't cancel, I will receive 6 brand-new novels every month and be billed just $4.99 per book in the U.S. or $5.49 per book in Canada. That's a saving of at least 17% off the cover price. It's quite a bargain! Shipping and handling is just 50¢ per book in the U.S. and 75¢ per book in Canada.* I understand that accepting the 2 free books and gifts places me under no obligation to buy anything. I can always return a shipment and cancel at any time. Even if I never buy another book, the two free books and gifts are mine to keep forever.

105/305 IDN GH5P

Name _____ (PLEASE PRINT) _____

Address _____ Apt. # _____

City _____ State/Prov. _____ Zip/Postal Code _____

Signature (if under 18, a parent or guardian must sign) _____

Mail to the **Reader Service:**
IN U.S.A.: P.O. Box 1867, Buffalo, NY 14240-1867
IN CANADA: P.O. Box 609, Fort Erie, Ontario L2A 5X3

**Are you a subscriber to Love Inspired® books
and want to receive the larger-print edition?
Call 1-800-873-8635 or visit www.ReaderService.com.**

* Terms and prices subject to change without notice. Prices do not include applicable taxes. Sales tax applicable in N.Y. Canadian residents will be charged applicable taxes. Offer not valid in Quebec. This offer is limited to one order per household. Not valid for current subscribers to Love Inspired books. All orders subject to credit approval. Credit or debit balances in a customer's account(s) may be offset by any other outstanding balance owed by or to the customer. Please allow 4 to 6 weeks for delivery. Offer available while quantities last.

Your Privacy—The Reader Service is committed to protecting your privacy. Our Privacy Policy is available online at www.ReaderService.com or upon request from the Reader Service.

We make a portion of our mailing list available to reputable third parties that offer products we believe may interest you. If you prefer that we not exchange your name with third parties, or if you wish to clarify or modify your communication preferences, please visit us at www.ReaderService.com/consumerchoice or write to us at Reader Service Preference Service, P.O. Box 9062, Buffalo, NY 14240-9062. Include your complete name and address.

LII5

SPECIAL EXCERPT FROM

Love Inspired

*When an Amish bachelor suddenly must care for a baby,
will his beautiful next-door neighbor rush to his aid?*

*Read on for a sneak preview of
THE AMISH MIDWIFE,
the final book in the brand-new trilogy
LANCASTER COURTSHIPS*

"I know I can't raise a baby. I can't! You know what to do.
You take her! You raise her." Joseph thrust Leah toward
Anne. The baby started crying.

"Don't say that. She is your niece, your blood. You
will find the strength you need to care for her."

"She needs more than my strength. She needs a
mother's love. I can't give her that."

Joseph had no idea what a precious gift he was trying
to give away. He didn't understand the grief he would feel
when his panic subsided. She had to make him see that.

Anne stared into his eyes. "I can help you, Joseph,
but I can't raise Leah for you. Your sister Fannie has
wounded you deeply, but she must have enormous faith
in you. Think about it. She could have given her child
away. She didn't. She wanted Leah to be raised by you,
in our Amish ways. Don't you see that?"

He rubbed a hand over his face. "I don't know what
to think."

"You haven't had much sleep in the past four days.
If you truly feel you can't raise Leah, you must go to
Bishop Andy. He will know what to do."

LIEXP1015

"He will tell me it is my duty to raise her. Did you mean it when you said you would help me?" His voice held a desperate edge.

"Of course. Before you make any rash decisions, let's see if we can get this fussy child to eat something. Nothing wears on the nerves faster than a crying *bubbel* that can't be consoled."

She took the baby from him.

He raked his hands through his thick blond hair again. "I must milk my goats and get them fed."

"That's fine, Joseph. Go and do what you must. Leah can stay with me until you're done."

"*Danki*, Anne Stoltzfus. You have proven you are a good neighbor. Something I have not been to you." He went out the door with hunched shoulders, as if he carried the weight of the world upon them.

Anne looked down at little Leah with a smile. "He'd better come back for you. I know where he lives."

Don't miss
THE AMISH MIDWIFE
by USA TODAY bestselling author Patricia Davids.
Available November 2015 wherever
Love Inspired® books and ebooks are sold.

LIEXP1015